# THE RIGHT HOOK

LARRY GAYTAN

Published by The Cornerstone Publishing.

ISBN:
Paperback: 979-8-9948250-1-3
eBook: 979-8-9948250-0-6

*This book is dedicated to my Aunt Lily.*

# Chapter 1

Lee had worked in the oil fields of West Texas for three years, since the day he graduated high school. It was a high paying job, but it wasn't steady work. One day you could be given a huge bonus, the next day you could be without a job. Everyone at the site knew what they were in for when they put in for the job. When the money was good, it was great. But when the government stepped in, things turned sour in a hurry.

At the end of his shift one day, Lee's co-workers told him to head into the office without looking him in the eye. Lee knew what was coming as he headed toward the rundown trailer at the end of the parking area of the job site. Walking up the stairs to the door, Lee hesitated as he removed his work gloves and put them in his back pocket. He understood, as all his coworkers did, the company was downsizing at their site. Another slowdown in oil production. As he opened the door, Lee saw his boss was on the phone.

Holding the receiver to his ear with one hand, his boss used his other hand to motion Lee towards an empty chair. Sitting down, Lee gazed out the window across the vastness of the oil fields. After a short conversation, his boss hung up the phone and began a stumbling explanation about the economy and cutbacks and how other guys had families, this was something he didn't want to do but he had been left with no choice. Although Lee paid little attention, he heard the bits about something to do with the oil industry slowing down and people having to be let go. After a few minutes, Lee shook his boss's hand with respect and accepted his last paycheck and the usual offer of return once the industry picked up again (although deep down Lee somehow knew he wouldn't be back next time).

Frustration and confusion set in as Lee exited the trailer and headed towards the drilling site. As he approached, his coworkers stopped what they were doing and turned to face him. Their clothes and faces were covered in the same oil stains that covered his own. From a work basket three stories up a snubbing unit, an older man stared down at Lee. Removing his hard hat and swallowing hard at the lump in his throat, Lee met the man's gaze and nodded. The man waved goodbye. A few moments later, Lee climbed into the bed of a pickup truck with the other men, friends who had also been terminated that day. As the truck peeled out of the parking area, particles of dust spun off its tires, joining the rest of the dust blowing in the West Texas wind.

✝

One week later, Lee's friends dropped him off at the bus station, somehow a little more worn and haggard. Lee had made the decision to spend some time with his mother in Boston, and given the partying that he and his friends had accomplished that week, he was happy that enough of his paycheck remained to cover a ticket. Lee got on the bus and made his way to the back of the bus and took a seat next to the window. The decision to leave Texas was still weighing heavily on his mind. Maybe he could find another oil site and keep making good money, sending some back home to his mom and helping her. Maybe his site would hire him back after a shorter time than he was thinking. Maybe. So many maybes.

He used his jacket as a pillow and leaned it against the window, making himself as comfortable as possible for the long journey ahead. He had so much going through his mind. He had left behind the only friends he had and the only work he knew how to do. He kept asking himself if he was making the right choice. All of these questions kept swirling through Lee's mind, keeping him from sleeping, but eventually he dozed off to the lull of the bus tires on the road.

Lee's body was so exhausted by the stress he was under and the hard work he had been putting it through for the last few years. Finally, his mind gave in, and he fell into a deep sleep, dreaming about his childhood when he and his best friend were 11 years old.

"Jack, let's go, we already have the wagon FULL of watermelons, and that one won't FIT!," said Lee.

It was the summer before sixth grade and almost every Saturday morning in July the two boys would pull Lee's Radio Flyer wagon through the neighborhood, collecting cans and bottles for money for candy or whatever other treasures they could find. To everyone in the neighborhood who saw the two boys, it was always a mission of no good. Today was one of those days.

One boy would pull the wagon while the other would push and try to hold the watermelons in place. They finally made it to the cotton field which was only about a mile away from Lee's house but today seemed like a million. There were about 5 acres next to the cotton fields that grew watermelons so Jack and Lee decided that a few from the edge wouldn't be missed at all.

The boys were going to take the watermelons and sell them for a few dollars each to make some spending money for the carnival coming to town in a couple of days. Lee had a weird feeling about taking the melons, his mother had always talked to him about stealing and how wrong it was, but Jack had convinced him that a few on the outside of the farmland wouldn't even be missed. Besides, Jack said, old man Gunther, who owned the farm, didn't even show up until lunchtime so no one would even know but the two boys.

"Come on, Jack. Just leave that one. We have plenty and it's too big anyway. The wagon is full already and it's going to be hard to pull," said Lee.

"Yeah, you're right. It is awfully big. I can hardly pick it up by myself. Maybe next time we should bring my wagon," replied Jack.

"Next time?" asked Lee. "I'm not doing this again. You said it was just this time for the carnival. Are you crazy? If old man Gunther catches us?"

Jack laughed. "You worry too much!"

Lee said, "This is wrong, Jack. Besides, what happens if we can't sell the watermelons? We can't hide them anywhere. We can't let our parents find out because old man Gunther knows them. Then what?"

Suddenly Jack yelled, "Old Man Gunther!"

Lee said, "I know, that's what I was saying..." Jack screamed, "No! He's coming! RUN!"

Jack's eyes were huge as he pointed to the west end of the farm. Sure enough, there was old man Gunther on his old tractor, chewing on a cigar, fist up in the air, headed their way.

The two boys looked at each other and yelled, "What do we do now?"

Just then, the bus lurched to a stop and Lee shot up and out of his deep sleep. He was sweating and his jacket was in a tight wad in his hands. He looked around to make sure no one noticed he had been dreaming and then smiled to himself as he remembered the rest of what a day that was! Lee was pretty sure his butt was still sore from the whippin' he had received.

Lee stepped off the bus for a stretch and realized they were already out of Texas. He hadn't understood just how tired he had been. The bus driver called everyone back on the bus and Lee took his seat in the back once again. As the bus started and the world passed by outside his window, Lee reflected more on his life in West Texas. He was still upset about how things had gone with the oil company, but he had a feeling that he was taking the first step of an important journey.

He reached into his duffle bag and took out his Bible. It was worn and had seen little of him the past few years. Holding his Bible in his hands, Lee realized that he was not yet ready to return to it. Instead, he removed the pictures from inside the front cover and put the Bible back in his bag. Some of the pictures showed him as a child with his family and with his best friend, while others were of his buddies at the oil field. His eyes began to tear up as he flipped through them. Returning them to his Bible, he put them back into his bag and began to look out the window again.

As the hours passed, the weather seemed to mirror his mood. Lee's thoughts were emotional throughout Arkansas as the grey rain was falling over North Little Rock. He still contemplated whether he was doing the right thing. There were moments he would stare at his cell phone, almost praying the job site would send him a text asking him to come back. In those moments, Lee was sure he would have without hesitation.

The bus ride took Lee through Tennessee, then Washington DC. Lee was tempted here to just hop off the bus and start new. There was so much to see and do here. But what would he be able to do? And in the land of politics, the people who put him out of a job in the first place. Then came New York, which was blanketed in a thick fog, literally nothing to see or do here, even if he would have had the time, he thought to himself. To Lee, the rain, fog and hail were all signs of the emotional trip he was taking.

When the bus finally reached Boston, it made its way through downtown to the station. As it did, Lee was able to see some things he had only heard about from those he knew who had done some traveling. His heart skipped a beat at the sight of Fenway Park, a definite Bucket List for Lee.

# Chapter 2

Once the bus reached the station, he exited quickly, grabbed his bag and hailed a cab. Climbing into the back seat, he handed the driver a piece of paper with his mother's address. Only two things were on Lee's mind now: hugging his mom and a nice, hot shower.

The cab arrived about 20 minutes later. As it pulled up, Lee saw an elderly woman kneeling to water some plants on a small front porch. At the sound of the cab door slamming, the woman straightened and turned around. Lee gazed into his mother's face. Then, as she smiled and tears filled her eyes, he approached her quickly, dropped his bag in the yard, and wrapped her in a hug.

"Sorry, I probably stink. I've been on the bus forever," Lee said.

His mom laughed. "You don't stink any more than I do. I've been outside in the sun watering the same plant all day waiting for you."

They both laughed, hugged each other again and headed inside. Lee's mom gave him a quick tour of the house. The wooden stairs squeaked as they climbed to the second floor. When she had shown him to his new bedroom, Lee's mother excused herself and headed back downstairs. As Lee entered the bedroom, he saw a twin-sized bed against the wall with a small lamp dresser next to it. As he dropped his duffle bag at the foot of the bed and sat down, he found a note on the pillow. He began to read.

Dear Lee,

I'm so glad you're here. Please make yourself at home. I know it's going to take some time to get used to being here, especially with me being your new roommate, but I promise I will do my best to help you feel comfortable. Son, don't hesitate to ask for anything. Again, I'm glad you're here. I love you, Lee."

Love Mom

Contemplating how he would adjust to his new town and to living with his mother again, Lee looked around the room. A rosary necklace hung from the wall above the bed. He stared at it for a moment, but then he grew frustrated and angry and stuffed it into the drawer of his nightstand. Exhausted, he yawned, stretched, and lay down.

He awoke the next morning to his mother knocking on his door and telling him loudly that breakfast was waiting downstairs when he was ready. As her footsteps receded down the stairs, he realized that he had fallen asleep in his clothes. Standing, he glanced out the window and saw a blue jay perched on the branch of a tree. The bird looked back at him for a moment, and then it flew away. From downstairs, he heard his mother calling his name. He laughed to himself as he remembered that "when you are ready" meant "now."

As Lee ate his breakfast, his mother rushed to pack her lunch and briefly explained that she would soon have to switch to the night shift at the hospital. She asked him if he could drop her off, saying that it might give him an opportunity to familiarize himself with the city. He agreed, and they left a few minutes later.

✝

When Lee arrived back home, he took a shower, got dressed, and began his day by unpacking his bag. He hung the pictures from inside his Bible from thumbtacks on the wall. Then, glancing briefly over the Bible, he stuck it into the drawer of his nightstand, next to the rosary then quickly shut the drawer. He knew his mother would want him to attend church with her on Sunday, so he needed to find a job quickly.

Downstairs on the couch, he opened a newspaper he had bought from a man at an intersection on his way home. He began thumbing through the classifieds, circling promising job opportunities. He spent the rest of his day making phone calls and setting up interviews for the coming week.

At the end of the week, Lee went to several interviews, but none had offered a job. He was growing frustrated and was starting to lose hope. After dropping off his mother one evening, he noticed two beautiful women walking into a local pub. He decided to stop in, and he took a seat at the bar next to them. They were giggling, and he saw this as an opportunity to spark a conversation with a joke.

"Hey ladies, do y'all want to hear a joke?" he asked.

"Why not?" one of them said as if it didn't really matter.

"Why don't sharks eat clowns?"

The women said nothing, but one of them raised an eyebrow, signaling that he should continue.

"Because they taste funny!" he said with a smile and a wink.

The women chuckled sarcastically, and then they stood up and walked away. One of them called back, "Nice one!"

"Whonk, whonk, whonk!" the bartender said with a laugh. "You must not be from around here."

"What makes you say that?" Lee asked, turning to face him.

"Well, the first thing is that shirt you're wearing—"

Lee looked down at his shirt, which read "Everything is Bigger in Texas!"

"—and the second is that lame joke you just told! By the way, my name is Gil."

"My name is Lee."

"So, are you from Texas?"

"I am. I've been working the oil fields for the last three years until I wasn't."

Their conversation continued over the course of the night, though it was periodically interrupted by the thirsty crowd. Lee told Gil how frustrating his week of job hunting had been. At one point, he said that he would do anything for work, even spend his days cleaning toilets. Gil paused for a moment. Then, he offered Lee a job that would change his life forever.

Two years later, Father Fred O'Connor was finishing his weekly class at Boston University, lecturing in his strong Irish accent.

"Referring to last week's lecture on sin and how it affects our daily lives, it affects the choices we make. We occasionally have an evil imagination and think that sins are arbitrary, and that "sin" will take the fun out of our daily lives. This is wrong to believe. We have a loving God who forgives us, and for the most part, we understand the difference between what is wrong and what is right. The scripture reveals a tug of war between sin and salvation. Ask yourself what you are struggling with today. Which side is tugging harder?"

"Alright class, that will be a great stopping point for now. Just remember, God hates sin, but—"

"God loves the sinner! Amen!" the class repeated with him.

As his students departed, Father O'Connor returned his books and his Bible to his briefcase. Peggy, his niece, who was also a student in the class, was waiting to walk out with him. As they stepped into the hallway, he put his arm around her and asked how she was doing.

"I'm doing well, thank you," she said, and told him that she had called her mother in Dublin. She then repeated to him the story that her mother had told her about how her father and Father O'Connor, his brother, went fishing on Sundays when they were young boys. As she told him the story, Father O'Connor smiled and chimed in with details.

"Your father was a little rascal, he was!" Father O'Connor said with a wink.

A little way down the hall, they ran into a professor who was a good friend of Father O'Connor's. Father O'Connor introduced Peggy, and then the two professors began a conversation. While they were talking, Peggy glanced out a window and saw two men running. The professors said goodbye soon after, and Peggy and her uncle left the building.

When they stepped outside, they saw two young men in university sweatshirts beating on a fellow student. With a concerned look on her face, Peggy asked her uncle what he thought they were fighting about.

"I don't know," Father O'Connor said, shaking his head. Then he and Peggy began moving cautiously to break up the fight.

# Chapter 3

Lee was sitting on a stool in the janitor's room repairing a disabled buffer when he heard a commotion echoing down the hall. Standing abruptly, he rushed down the hall and shoved open the doors at the rear of the building.

Outside, a student was being attacked by two other students. Reacting quickly, Lee pushed one of the attackers off the man. In response, the other attacker turned towards Lee and aimed a left jab at his head. Lee ducked the punch easily, and as he rose, he threw an uppercut under the man's outstretched arm. It landed solidly on his chin, and he crumpled in a heap to the ground.

By this time, the man Lee had pushed aside had regained his footing. He stepped forward and threw a left hook at Lee's jaw. Lee ducked again, but as he did, he landed a right hook just below the man's eye. The man fell backwards, landing heavily next to his friend.

"Get out of here, before I report both of you for ganging up on people!" Lee shouted at them.

As they rose slowly to their feet and began to flee, Lee noticed Peggy and Father O'Connor move from behind him. Father O'Connor knelt by the man who had been attacked and asked if he was okay, and Peggy handed him his backpack and books. Then, she turned to Lee and asked if he was alright.

Lee was still out of breath and did not respond. Instead, he turned and walked back through the doors of the building. At this moment, seeing Father O'Connor standing there having seen the incident, Lee was afraid he would lose his job for fighting on campus.

Once the doors had closed behind Lee, Peggy looked at her uncle, confused. Turning back to the student and helping him to his feet, Father O'Connor asked if he knew the gentlemen who had helped him. The student replied he did not know the man. Then, he shouldered his backpack, thanked Father O'Connor and Peggy, and walked away.

The following Sunday morning, Lee decided to go to the church a few blocks away from his mother's house. He hadn't stepped inside one in quite a while and was hesitant to do so as he stood on the front steps of the old wooden building. He had always felt the hand he had been dealt in life was an unfair one, even the choice of having to move to Boston, but he knew God had already lay his path before him. Lee just had to make the choices.

Lee made his way inside the cathedral. It was stunning. The stained glass, the height of the ceiling, the size Lee didn't notice from the outside. He began to think of his childhood and how the church was where his family was last together in Texas. He had been an altar boy. Things were happy.

The choir began to sing, and Lee remembered being a boy and sitting and watching the choir sing. Listening to the harmony and the words and not quite understanding it all but feeling how beautiful it all was and how safe he felt. Lee sat in a pew and began to feel that same serenity and peacefulness come over him.

Lee listened until the choir finished. As he looked around, he was overwhelmed once again at the beauty of the cathedral. Then he heard an Irish accent coming from the pulpit as he turned to face it. The priest began his sermon.

Lee became uneasy. The past and the present were colliding in his mind and heart once again. He wanted to be there listening, but his mind kept telling him he didn't belong. Finally, Lee quietly stood from the pew and left the cathedral and headed home.

✝

One week later, Lee waited in the hall with his mop bucket for a class to finish. Once the students had left the auditorium, he entered, put in his earphones, and began to mop.

Having knelt behind a chair to pick up some papers that had fallen out of her notebook, Peggy rose and saw Lee cleaning. Although she was anxious about approaching him, once she reached the floor of the auditorium, she stepped forward and tentatively tapped him on the back of his shoulder.

Startled, Lee turned around quickly. Recognizing her, he removed his earphones and said, "I'm sorry. I didn't know you were in the classroom. I'll get out of your way and come back later."

"No, no, please forgive me," she said. "I didn't mean to startle you."

"Then can I help you with something?"

When she mentioned the fight the week before, Lee was initially afraid that she had reported him to the campus police. However, he relaxed somewhat when she asked him why he had helped the man, whom she discovered Lee did not know.

"I'm sorry," he replied, "but I have a lot of work to do and don't really have time to talk. Excuse me."

"Of course," Peggy said. Although she was more curious than ever, she left him to his work and left the auditorium.

✝

The next day, Father O'Connor met Peggy for lunch after class. As they chatted about their day, he got the feeling that something was bothering her. She seemed detached, and she was staring out the window as if in a daydream. As she began to eat, a thought crossed Father O'Connor's mind.

✝

Later that day, after he had finished his last class of the week, Father O'Connor decided to visit the College of Education. After strolling through the building, he stopped outside a cracked door, above which hung a sign reading "Janitor Room." Tapping lightly, he called, "Hello? Is anyone in there?"

When he received no response, he pushed open the door and walked slowly in. No one appeared to be in the small room, but he noticed a broken-down buffer surrounded by nuts and bolts. Recognizing the work underway, he searched the nearby table for the right tool. He soon realized the tool he was looking for was not there, but he did find what seemed to be an awkward, jerry-rigged replacement. Returning to the buffer, he wiped some of the dust from it with his finger and found the label that showed the make and model on it. Then he left the room and walked out of the building.

✝

A few days later, Peggy waited anxiously at her desk for her class to let out, her gaze fixed on the minute hand of the clock at the front of the auditorium. She hoped to run into Lee again, and she thought of what she might say to him if she did. She removed a small mirror from her purse and used it to fix her hair. When the professor announced that class was done for the day, she stayed at her desk until everyone had left. A few minutes later, Lee entered with his trash cart. Standing, Peggy walked down to the front of the auditorium and approached him.

"So, are we going to be running into each other like this all the time?" he said, removing his earphones.

"Only if you keep brushing me off," she responded.

They exchanged introductions, but Lee felt uneasy. He did not understand why she was so persistent in getting to know him, and he was introverted and generally uncomfortable in conversations, especially with people he thought would not be interested in speaking with him. He told her very little about himself, but Peggy was not so shy. She told him that she was from Dublin, Ireland, but was living with her uncle while she finished her master's degree at the University. Eventually, he told her that he had to get back to work, and they parted ways.

✝

Leaning into the refrigerator, Father O'Connor made a list of what they would need from the grocery store. Once he had finished, he yelled upstairs at Peggy to ask if she needed a break from studying and would like to go with him. She yelled back she would, and they left a few minutes later.

At the store, Father O'Connor asked Peggy if everything was going well at school. When she responded that it was, he asked if she had spoken to the young janitor.

Smiling, Peggy replied that his name was Lee and that he was from Texas. When she had provided a few more details, he asked if she would like to invite him over for dinner the next time she talks to him. Although her expression was surprised, the idea elated her.

# Chapter 4

The next week, Peggy once again waited anxiously for her class to finish and, when it did, she took her time gathering her books and putting them in her backpack. When the other students had left the auditorium, there was still no sign of Lee. She waited for a few more minutes, and then she left, disappointed. On her way out of the building, she stopped at the janitor room. The door was wide open. Nervously, she knocked lightly on the molding. There was no response.

Realizing that Lee was not there, she walked in slowly and looked around. Near the disabled buffer on the worktable, a small flyer caught her eye. It advertised an amateur boxing match, and it listed the grand prize of five thousand dollars.

She turned to leave just as Lee walked into the room.

"What are you doing?" he asked, looking at her cautiously. "Why are you in here?"

Flustered, Peggy explained that she had waited for him after class, but since he had never hadn't shown up, she had come here looking for him.

"What do you need with me?" he asked.

Sensing his exasperation, she decided to be more direct. She did not want him to end the conversation before she had a chance to ask him to dinner. She told him that Father O'Connor was her uncle, and he had asked her to invite him to dinner on Friday.

"Why?" he asked, giving her a strange look.

Thinking quickly, she explained that it would be good for him to get out and to have a home-cooked meal. She told him it would beat the junk food he had on his worktable. Smiling, she wrote her address on a piece of paper and handed it to him. Then, she told him she and her uncle would not take "no" for an answer and if he did not show, he would have an angry Irish woman in his janitors room every day until he said "yes." Then she turned and walked out of the room, not allowing Lee to see the smile on her lips or the blush on her cheeks.

"What time should I show up?" Lee yelled after her.

Her smile widened when she realized he would come, but she hid it as she turned around. "Seven o'clock!" she told him. Then she turned and almost ran down the hall with excitement.

Lee smiled to himself as he looked at the paper Peggy had left.

✝

At five minutes to seven Friday evening, Lee climbed out of a cab at the address Peggy had given him. Holding a pastry box in one hand, he rang the doorbell with the other.

Opening the door, Peggy was surprised to see Lee in faded jeans and a blue, fitted sports jacket over a white T-shirt. She had never seen him in anything but his janitor clothes. The color rose in her cheeks again as she caught herself staring. "You clean up well!" she said out loud. Then, noticing the box in his hand, she said, "Oh! How sweet! But you really didn't have to bring anything."

"My mother would kill me if I came empty-handed. Besides, it's just a little something," he replied with a smile.

Peggy led Lee through the living room and into the kitchen, where Father O'Connor was just finishing the dishes. She introduced the two and they shook hands. Then, Father O'Connor offered Lee a seat and joined him at the kitchen table, which was spread with Dublin Coddle. On one plate was heaped Irish sausage, bacon, onions, and sliced potatoes, and on another was soda bread and colcannon. Peggy put the dessert box next to the colcannon, poured them all iced tea, and then took her place at the table.

Father O'Connor asked if Lee would like to say grace.

"Sure, I can do that," Lee responded slowly.

The three of them joined hands, and then Lee began to pray. "Thank you, Lord, for the food you have blessed us with and the hands that prepared it. God, thank you for this dish from Ireland and this tea from Boston. Amen."

Although Peggy's and Father O'Connor's eyes stayed shut, they both wore small grins. "Amen," they repeated. As Peggy served the food, Father O'Connor struck up a conversation with Lee.

"Peggy says you're from West Texas," he said.

"Yes sir, a town called Lubbock," Lee replied.

"What brings you to Boston?"

"Well, I used to work in the oil fields back home, but in recent years, the oil companies have been downsizing. They had to let me go. I decided to come here and spend some time with my mother."

"Oh, your mother lives here?"

"Yes sir, she's a nurse. I've been living here for two years already."

Noticing that Lee's plate had gotten a little empty, Peggy asked if he would like some more.

"Just a little more," he said, so Peggy dished him another spoonful of Dublin Coddle.

"Do you like your work as a janitor?" Father O'Connor asked.

"Yes sir. It's a job, and I am very grateful for it."

"I visited the janitor room at the College of Education a couple of days ago, but you weren't in. However, I did find a buffer on the table didn't seem to be working, and I noticed that you didn't have the tool you needed to work on it."

"Yes sir. I lent the tool to a friend, but he moved out of town, and I forgot to get it back. If I report it lost or stolen, I could lose my job."

"I think I might have the tool you need in my garage."

Lee started, nearly spilling his tea down his shirt. "Really?" he said. "Are you kidding me?"

"Believe it or not, I was in charge of a maintenance department before I was ordained. In that position, I learned how to work on those kinds of buffers. I can lend you the tool if you promise to return it."

Happy and surprised, Lee asked, "Can we get it right now?"

Peggy smiled as she listened to Lee and her uncle talk. Father O'Connor smiled, too. "Sure," he said, "as soon as we find out what's in this white box you brought."

"I hope you guys like pecan pie," Lee said, opening the box.

"It's Peggy's favorite dessert," Father O'Connor said, as Peggy's smile widened.

"Well, I hope she likes it," Lee said, looking at Peggy. "I made it earlier."

"You made this?" she asked.

"I sure did, and it's the only pie I know how to make," Lee said with a laugh. "When I was a young boy back in Texas, my parents used to have a pecan tree in our backyard. My dad made me pick up all the pecans so my mother could make this pie. After a few years of watching her make it, I just learned how she did it."

"Oh! I know what will go great with this," Peggy said, standing and walking to the refrigerator. She returned with a can of whipped cream.

"You can't put that on yet," Lee said.

"Why not?"

"Because you still have the cap on."

Peggy smiled sarcastically and removed the cap. They continued their conversation as they ate the pie. When they had finished, Peggy cleared the dishes and cleaned the table while Father O'Connor and Lee went to the garage for the tool.

Father O'Connor opened the side door of the garage, flipped on the lights, and walked in, heading straight to the back for the tool that Lee would need to fix the buffer. He began rooting through a bin next to a pile of fishing supplies, including nets, life jackets, and tackle boxes. Above these, several fishing poles hung from a rack on the wall.

Lee followed for a few steps before stopping in awe. The wall opposite him was full of trophies, medals, plaques, and pictures. Among them was an old pair of boxing gloves. An old punching bag hung from the middle of the ceiling, and beside it was weights, jump ropes, and an old pair of boxing shoes. Lee drifted towards the wall of trophies. As he got closer, he noticed that while they were covered in dust, they were all engraved with Father O'Connor's name.

Father O'Connor was bent over, looking for the tool and making a lot of noise. As he searched, Lee walked slowly along the wall. Among the photos, he saw pictures of Father O'Connor with Muhammad Ali and Sugar Ray Leonard. He also saw an old picture of a young kid in a boxing stance standing beside a much younger Father O'Connor.

"I found it!" Father O'Connor said, turning around with the tool.

"Great!" Lee replied. "You used to be a boxer, Father O'Connor? With all of these medals, trophies, and pictures, you must have been a great one."

Father O'Connor smiled modestly. "Son, I wouldn't say I was a great boxer, but in those days, I was okay," he said.

"Well, not to sound disrespectful of what you've done with your life—I mean being a priest and all—but what made you stop boxing?"

Father O'Connor's expression grew thoughtful, and he sat down on a stool. After a moment of silence, he told Lee the story of his last fight. He had knocked out his opponent and watched as the man fell in an awkward position.

"He ended up paralyzed," Father O'Connor said softly, his eyes full of sadness. "Because of me." He then explained after that, he could no longer bring himself to enter a boxing ring. He said after a very long period of prayer, he had decided to devote the rest of his life to serving the Lord.

In that moment, a memory flashed before Lee's eyes. He was a child in Texas, and he and his best friend were playing with some other children on the merry-go-round at school. Before the memory could progress, Lee shook his head to clear it. It was gone as quickly as it had appeared.

"Are you okay, son?" Father O'Connor asked.

"Yes, yes, I'm fine," Lee said. "Well, I had better get going. Thank you, Father. I will return this tool to you soon." With that, Lee turned and walked quickly out of the garage.

Father O'Connor stood and walked to the doorway. As he watched Lee walk away, he wondered what had bothered him and which part of their conversation had sparked it.

# Chapter 5

The following Sunday, Lee went for a run early in the morning. He had developed a regular route, but that day he had decided to run through a neighborhood that had a park with a lake. The weather was perfect. Even though there was light fog, he could see the lake in the distance. It was encircled by trees, and the shade they cast made the path at their feet seem endless.

He ran at a steady pace, and he had made it almost the whole way around the lake before he noticed the man. He was wearing a hat, and he was sitting in a chair with a book in his lap and a fishing pole propped beside him in a pole stand. Lee slowed his pace, and the fog seemed to vanish as he got closer. Able to see the man more clearly, Lee realized it was Father O'Connor.

He stopped running and bent over with his hands on his knees, catching his breath. Straightening slowly, he wondered whether he should stop and say "hello." He decided he should, and he began to walk towards Father O'Connor.

At the sound of footsteps, Father O'Connor looked up from his book.

"Good morning, Father!" Lee called.

"Oh! Good morning to you! What brings you here?"

"I run every Sunday morning, but never on this side of town. Something told me to run a different route today."

"Well, it's beautiful this morning," Father O'Connor replied. Both looked out across the lake.

"So, you come here often to fish and read?"

"Oh, I do! I love the scenery, and I love spending time out here reading my Bible and praying, especially that I'll catch the big fish!" Father O'Connor said with a little laugh. Tightening the line on the fishing rod, he said, "The other night when we were talking in the garage, I couldn't stop thinking something was bothering you. Why don't you have a seat beside me so we can talk, if you don't mind?"

Lee sat down, but he remained silent and continued to stare out across the lake.

After a few moments, Father O'Connor continued. "Lee, whatever it is you are holding inside is not good for your heart. If you need to talk about something, I'm here to listen."

Lee could not say exactly what it was, but something about Father O'Connor reminded him of his father, who was back home in Texas. Perhaps it was his wisdom. Whatever it was, however, Lee felt comfortable opening up to Father O'Connor. He explained when he was a child, there was an accident on the merry-go-round at school. As he told the story, every memory was as clear as if the accident had happened yesterday.

"I was in the sixth grade, and it was a Friday, about forty-five minutes before school let out," he began. "Mrs. Sanchez was our teacher. She had told us if we behaved the whole day, we would be able to go outside and play thirty minutes before the end of class. So, we were on our best behavior that whole day, and we got to go outside and play. My friends and I were at the merry-go-round. Some of the girls in our class liked to be pushed on it, rather than doing the pushing themselves. My best friend, Jack, and I wanted to push the merry-go-round at the same time, but that was hard to do. So, Jack and I got into an argument about who was going to push the girls. We got in each other's faces, and I got so mad that I pushed him down. Jack got up quick, and he came at me. We fell to the floor and rolled around, trying to punch each other. I finally got on top of him, and I punched him in the head because he was covering his face with his hands. Mrs. Sanchez pulled me off of him, but as she escorted us to the office, I saw that Jack was bleeding from his ear."

Lee took a deep breath and continued to tell the story to Father O'Connor. "I remember being in the principal's office and thinking to myself that I had just gotten into a fight with my best friend over something really stupid. I couldn't believe it. When we were free to go, we waited for our parents to pick us up and we didn't say one word to each other. We didn't even hang out that weekend."

Lee sat quietly for a moment. Although he and Father O'Connor were both staring out over the lake, each saw an entirely different scene in their mind's eye. Lee resumed his story.

"Before class began on Monday, I waited for Jack to arrive so I could apologize to him. The bell rang, but Jack's desk was empty. Then, Mrs. Sanchez came in and closed the door."

Lee's eyes filled with tears and his body began to shake. Father O'Connor put his hand on Lee's shoulder and said, "take your time" shortly Lee continued his story.

"She told the class that she had an announcement to make. You could see she was struggling. Finally, she said, 'One of our students will not be in class anymore.' I knew right then that she was talking about Jack. At first, I hoped they had moved him to a different class, but then Mrs. Sanchez said, 'Jack was in the hospital this weekend and passed away suddenly.'

"One of my classmates asked how, but I knew. I knew before she had even said anything that my friend was gone. Then, Mrs. Sanchez said, 'Jack suffered and died from a brain aneurism. His brain was bleeding and they couldn't stop it.'"

Lee swallowed hard, trying to control his emotions. "I couldn't believe what I had just heard. I began to panic and cry. I tried to put my head down on my desk, but I just couldn't take it. I ran out of the classroom and down the hall to the bathroom. I threw up, and then I sat in the corner and cried. I knew it was all my fault."

Father O'Connor turned his chair so that he could face Lee.

Lee remained silent for a few moments, trying to gather himself. Then he said, "For several years, I didn't talk to anyone, not even my parents. I'm pretty sure I was the reason they got a divorce." Lee dropped his head into his hands.

"Lee, what happened to Jack was not your fault. Your parents' divorce was not your fault," Father O'Connor said, slowly and softly.

Lee wiped his eyes and continued to look out over the lake, quietly.

"God had a plan for Jack. He needed him at that moment. He has a plan for you, as well. You can't live in the past or let it define who you are or who you become. Worry comes from the devil, and you have to trust in the Lord, son. Ask yourself, Lee, how long has it been since you put your trust in God?"

Then, Father O'Connor recited a passage from scripture, Psalm 34:18. "The Lord is close to the brokenhearted and saves those who are crushed in spirit," he said. "In a friendship, it is vital to put your friend first. I believe that you genuinely cared for Jack because you have been brokenhearted for quite some time. Now, it's time for the Lord to lift your spirits, and I think Jack would want that for you." There was another long pause as both men stared continuously at the lake.

Moments later, Lee wiped away his tears and stood up. Then, he extended his hand to shake Father O'Connor's hand. "Thank you for listening," he said. "I have never shared that with anyone. My parents struggled for years to get me to talk about that day, but I just never would. I never could, I guess. But thank you, especially for helping me to see the bigger picture, that I was not the one in control that day. I better get going, Father."

"Goodbye, Lee," Father O'Connor said. As he watched Lee walk away, he said a silent prayer for the young man.

On his way out of the park, Lee saw a blue jay on the branch of a nearby tree. He smiled to himself, feeling that the appearance of blue jays was somehow important in his life. The bird flew away, and Lee turned back to Father O'Connor. After a final wave, he began his run back home.

# Chapter 6

Later that evening after dropping his mother off at work that night, Lee slumped up the stairs to his room, exhausted. He had thought all day about his conversation with Father O'Connor. Lying on his bed, he turned his gaze to the drawer of his nightstand. After a few moments, he opened the drawer and took out his Bible. Holding the Bible on his chest, he looked up at one of the pictures hanging on the wall. It showed he and Jack as kids. "I have to move on. It was His will, not my doing," he said to himself.

Lee uttered a small, silent prayer and then said aloud, "Lord, give me the strength to be strong on this new journey that I begin with you." Then, he opened his Bible.

As Lee began to read, his eyes filled with tears, slowly cascading down his face and falling onto the pages. He knew the only way he could move forward was to let his past be his past and to trust in God. It had been so long since he had strayed from his faith. He closed the Bible and returned it to the drawer. As he did, his eyes fell upon the rosary. He kissed it and clutched it tightly to his chest. Then, closing his eyes, he drifted off to sleep.

✝

The next day, Lee felt like a new man. It was as though a huge weight had been lifted from his shoulders. He spent the morning fixing the buffer, using the tool Father O'Connor had lent him. As he reached for the wrench he would need to tighten the final bolts, his eyes found the flyer for the boxing match.

Hearing a knock at the door, he said, "come in" and turned.

"Hey, how are you doing?" Peggy asked, standing in the doorway.

"I'm doing good. I'm just about to finish putting this buffer back together," he said, tightening the final bolt.

"So, the tool my uncle lent you was useful?" Peggy asked, walking over and standing beside him.

"Very useful," he replied, smiling. "I'm about to turn it on to see if it works."

"Oh, it won't work."

"Why not?" Lee asked, confused.

"It's not plugged in," Peggy said in her Irish accent, pointing at the buffer's dangling cord.

Lee looked where Peggy was pointing, and then he looked back at her. They stared at each other for a moment, and then they both laughed. It had only been a short while and Lee was discovering they had the same sense of humor. Lee got up and plugged the cord into an outlet. He told Peggy to stand back, explaining he was not sure what the buffer would do. He was able to fix machines, he told her, but they were usually tied to the oil industry, not janitorial work.

In her anticipation and excitement, Peggy grabbed Lee's hand. At first, Lee's attention to the buffer kept him from noticing what he was holding. When he did notice, he smiled. Peggy noticed at the same time, and she smiled, too, blushing. Then, very slowly, they let go of each other's hand.

"Okay, here goes nothing!" Lee said, flipping the switch. The buffer whirred to life. "It works!" he exclaimed. He was happy knowing his job would be easier from now on, but he was also relieved. He had been afraid if the buffer had not started, he would have let Peggy down.

Peggy smiled, happy for Lee. Out of the corner of her eye, she noticed a piece of paper blow off the table and onto the floor. Stooping to pick it up, she recognized it as the flyer for the amateur boxing match. Having turned off the machine, Lee turned to face her.

"Are you planning to enter?" she asked, her smile fading slightly, a look of concern now on her face.

"No, I've never boxed a day in my life. I only took it because I could use the money. It was just a passing thought, and it's probably not for me." Changing the subject, he said, "I want to apologize for the other night. You know, for not saying goodbye to you and thanking you for inviting me to dinner."

"No worries, it was our pleasure. And we truly appreciated that you came."

Looking at Lee, Peggy sensed a change had occurred. It was more than he had finally gotten the buffer working; his smile was different, and he seemed happier and more talkative than she had ever seen him. This made her even happier to be close to him, so much so she completely forgot why she had come to see him in the first place. In fact, it did not matter anymore. The way he smiled at her made everything else fade away.

Peggy caught herself staring and blushed again. "Well, I had better let you get back to your work," she said. "I have to get to my next class now, anyway."

"Okay," he said, still smiling. "Thank you again for dinner the other night and tell your uncle I'll be returning his tool soon." As he watched her go, Lee realized how happy he felt whenever he was around her.

✝

The next week, Lee decided to visit Father O'Connor in his office after work. He wanted to thank him for letting him borrow the tool and to tell him how well it had worked. More importantly, he wanted to thank him for what he had said at the lake.

He wanted to tell Father O'Connor he had recognized the lingering effects Jack's death had had on him for long, and he now understood the memory of it was keeping him from being the man he should be. Lee wanted to tell him that, deep down, he had known this for a long time and what Father O'Connor had told him had finally brought him a great sense of peace.

He arrived at the College of Theology just as Father O'Connor was walking down the front steps, and Lee walked up to meet him.

"How are you doing, son?" Father O'Connor asked, a big smile on his face.

"Hello, Father. I'm fine, thank you," Lee said, shaking his hand. "I'm glad I ran into you. Do you have a minute?"

"Sure. Let's walk this way," Father O'Connor said, gesturing down the steps toward a path leading to the parking lot. "What's on your mind?" They found a bench and decided to stop and have a seat there.

"First of all, here's your tool, as promised. It was exactly what I needed," Lee said with a smile, handing Father O'Connor the tool. "Thank you. The buffer works better than ever."

"That's great. I'm glad it helped," Father O'Connor said, smiling back.

"I also wanted to tell you that I really appreciated the talk we had at the lake that morning," Lee said, his smile fading into a serious expression. "I can't stop thinking about why I took a different route that day. It's like something guided me towards that path and towards you. Whatever it was, I'm glad you were there, Father. It really helped me out. I feel more at peace now, as if a weight has been lifted from my shoulders. I know now God has a plan for me. I don't know what it is yet, but I know He wanted to help me unburden myself of my past. It wasn't just Him, though. He sent me to you. It was you, too, and I want to thank you for that."

"Don't thank me. It really was all God's doing," Father O'Connor replied, still smiling. "I am a messenger for Him, but he is the only one who knows your path. I truly believe it was the Holy Spirit that led you to the lake that day. It's the Holy Spirit who is going to help you to heal your relationship with God. But first, He needed you to understand that Jack's death was not your fault. Now, He will help you to see the bigger picture. All things happen for a reason, and we must not question these reasons. When you make God bigger than yourself, than your problems, than anything, then your problems get smaller and soon your worries will diminish. The key is to have faith and to trust in Him."

Lee looked away, contemplating Father O'Connor's words. As he did, he saw a blue jay land on a bush just a few feet from where they were sitting.

"Such a beautiful and majestic bird," Father O'Connor said. "I've seen that blue jay quite a bit lately. I sense that it's trying to tell me something."

Although Lee had also been seeing the blue jay, he did not want to hold up Father O'Connor and decided to stay quiet. Silence hung between them as they admired the bird. Then, just as quickly as it had appeared, the blue jay flew away.

Father O'Connor rose slowly from the bench and turned to face Lee. "Son," he said, "the biggest mistake we can make in our lives is to not have a relationship with God. There are many times in our lives when we think we do not need Him, but trust me, we do. All of us."

Lee looked up at Father O'Connor, and then he started to stand.

"I hope to see you around, Lee," Father O'Connor said. "I think God knows we have more to talk about. Have a blessed day." He winked, as if he knew something Lee did not.

"You too, Father," Lee said, slowly and softly. He was already pondering the meaning of Father O'Connor's parting words.

# Chapter 7

One week later, Lee ran into Peggy after her class and asked if she would be willing to meet with him for a moment after he got off work. He was getting out early that day, and he knew it would only take a second to say what he wanted to say.

She replied that she would be at the coffee shop down the road, and she gave him her phone number. "In case you get lost," she said.

✝

At the coffee shop, Peggy was excited that Lee wanted to meet with her. She opened her compact and checked her hair, and then she arranged and rearranged the items on the table. She also remembered something her uncle had said: Lee looked happier and that he appeared to be a truly genuine man. Peggy knew her uncle was a good judge of character, and she never doubted him. He was a priest, after all, and life had taught him to read people. Reaching into her purse, she remembered something else. Her uncle had said Lee might need a good friend to talk to sometimes. After all, he had said, it didn't seem as though Lee had many friends here. She had known what her uncle was insinuating, but she had not let on that she knew. Instead, she politely nodded and changed the subject. She didn't intend to let her uncle know just how interested in Lee she was just yet.

To pass the time and distract herself from how nervous she was, she tried to concentrate on her book. It was not easy, especially since she was on her third cup of coffee. Through the window by her table, she saw Lee walk to the door and into the coffee shop.

Spotting her, he smiled and waved.

"Hello, Lee!" Peggy said as he reached her table.

"Hi! Thanks again for meeting me. Is this where you hang out?" he asked, looking around. A few students were in line to order, but otherwise, the shop was mostly empty.

"Oh, not really. They have free Wi-Fi, though, and cappuccinos are half off today," she said, pointing at her cup. "This is my third one!" She laughed nervously. Lee's eyes opened wide as he said, "Oh, ok then I guess I won't order you another one just yet."

The bell on the door rang as customers came and went, but Lee paid no attention. He had asked Peggy to meet him for one reason. This reason required him to muster his nerve, however, so he began with small talk, fidgeting with a napkin that was on the table before he got there.

"Peggy, have you ever asked yourself why you were put here on earth? I mean, the reason God put you here?" Lee asked sincerely.

Taking a sip from her cappuccino, Peggy rested her cup gently on the table. She thought for a moment before responding. "I have actually thought about that often. I ask God to put me where he wants me to be, not where I might want to be. Why do you think you were put here on earth? What do you think your purpose is?"

"To be honest, I don't have a clue. I feel like I'm just learning to live day by day," Lee said with a small grin. After a moment, he continued. "I remember when I was a kid, me and my best friend, Jack, used to love to draw. We thought we were going to be famous artists one day. At least, I knew Jack could have been. Jack loved drawing birds, and his favorite was the blue jay. There was something special about the blue jay to him."

Peggy listened, smiling.

Just as Lee saw his opportunity, the waitress arrived to take his order. With a sigh, he asked for a glass of water and thanked her.

"You don't want a cappuccino?" Peggy asked. "They are really good here!"

"I can see that, but no thank you," Lee said with a laugh. "I don't drink anything with caffeine."

"Oh! I'm so sorry!" Peggy said, blushing. "Had I known; I would have suggested somewhere else for us to meet. Speaking of, what was it you wanted to talk to me about?"

"Oh no! I didn't mean to offend you!" Lee said. "I didn't really care where we met, so long as you agreed to meet with me." He laughed nervously and then continued. "Well, I've been thinking since you invited me to dinner a couple of weeks ago, I wanted to ask you if I can take you out to dinner this time. And I won't take 'no' for an answer," he said with uncertainty in his voice, "because I am a stubborn Texan who will show up at your house every day until you say 'yes.'"

Lee looked down at the napkin he had torn apart and laughed. Peggy sat quietly for a moment, and then she laughed, too. Although she looked calm on the outside, her stomach was in knots, and her heart was beating fast. She was happy he had finally asked her out. She wanted to jump for joy and scream "yes!" but she somehow kept her composure.

Finally, in a very calm voice, she said, "Sure. That is very kind of you. So, is this like a date? Because my uncle was actually the person who invited you originally and it would be kind of weird. Because if you are asking the person who invited you to dinner, it would be him..."

Lee could see that Peggy was nervous and excited, so he interrupted her before she could continue. "Yes ma'am," he said. "Where I come from, we call that a date. Is that okay? I mean, if we need to invite your uncle, I guess we can..." His smile widened. He hoped she knew he was teasing her. "Will Friday night be okay?"

"Sure," she said, smiling demurely, "and I will let my uncle know it's just going to be the two of us this time."

"Can I pick you up at seven?" he asked. He had an urge to jump out of his seat and hug her.

"Yes," she said, nodding and smiling.

Soon after, Lee said he needed to get going and Peggy said she needed to get some more studying done. They said goodbye. Lee made his way home, elated, and Peggy finished her cappuccino, her smile never leaving her face. Both of them were on cloud nine.

✝

On Friday afternoon, Lee could not wait until seven o'clock. He bought Peggy flowers after work, and then he went straight home to get ready. He wanted things to go really well, so as soon as Peggy had agreed to have dinner with him, he had made a reservation at a fancy Italian restaurant she had mentioned. Peggy had said that she had never been there, but she would love to try it some day.

When it was time for him to pick her up, he apologized once again to his mother for having to drop her off early.

"If it were for any other reason, I might be perturbed," she said with a laugh. "You're going on a date! You don't know how happy that makes me!"

# Chapter 8

Lee pulled up in front of Peggy's house promptly at seven. Before he got out of the car, he smiled into the rearview to make sure that nothing was stuck in his teeth. Then, he walked up the steps with Peggy's flowers in his left hand. He wanted to be able to shake Father O'Connor's hand if he answered the door.

As he was about to ring the doorbell, Peggy opened the door. Lee stared in stunned silence at the beautiful woman standing before him. She wore a black, strapless dress, a shawl, black high heels, and a necklace full of white diamond pearls. She looked amazing.

"I had a good time," he whispered, hardly able to speak because of her beauty.

Barely able to hear him, Peggy looked at him, confused. "I'm sorry?" she said. "What did you just say? Are those lovely flowers for me?"

Snapping out of her spell, Lee said "yes" with a hint of embarrassment. He handed her the flowers.

Peggy admired the flowers with a smile and then said, "Let me put them in a vase. Do you mind coming in for just a moment?"

Lee waited in the doorway while she put the flowers in water. A short time later, she returned, picked up her pocketbook from the table in the hallway, and said, "I'm ready."

"Great!" Lee said, having regained most of his composure. "Oh, by the way, is your uncle here? I didn't want to be rude and not say hi to him."

"No," Peggy said. "He just stepped out for a little bit."

They smiled at each other and then walked out. While Peggy locked the door behind them, Lee walked to the car and opened the passenger door. Before Peggy got in, she looked up and thanked him. He asked himself if her eyes had always been so intoxicating.

Closing the door after her, Lee circled the car and got in. Before he could turn the key, Peggy asked him, "Why did you say, 'I had a good time' at the doorstep?"

"I said it then in case I forget to tell you later."

Peggy looked into Lee's piercing eyes and smiled. It rained lightly as they drove, and the streetlights were reflected in the puddles.

Somehow, they found a parking spot right in front of the restaurant. This was pure luck for Lee because it had started to rain hard and Lee had not thought to bring an umbrella. Before they got out of the car, he suggested that they get into the restaurant as quickly as they could. "I'll do my best!" she said, looking down at her high heels.

Lee told her to stay where she was, and then he got out of the car and ran around to open her door. As she stepped out, he held his jacket over her head to shield her from the rain. She closed the door behind her, and they walked quickly into the restaurant.

When they had made it inside, Peggy noticed that it was very busy. Lee asked her to wait for a moment while he checked their reservation, and then he headed off through the crowd. When he returned a few minutes later, he did not look happy.

"You won't believe what happened," he said. "They mixed up our reservation."

"No problem," she said. "How long will it be until we are seated?"

"Well, they said the wait will be two hours."

When she heard this, Peggy smiled and shrugged. "Okay, I guess we'll wait?" she asked, clearly uncertain whether they should stay or go. The people around them looked nervously at each other, clearly hoping that their reservations were safe.

Feeling bad about the possibility of making Peggy wait for two hours, Lee looked out the window to see if it was still raining. As he did, he saw another, smaller restaurant across the street. It was by no means fancy. It looked like an old-school diner, and there did not seem to be many customers.

"Look across the street," he said, pointing. "Should we wait here for two hours, or should we try that restaurant?"

"Let's try it!" Peggy said, smiling. "It looks great to me!"

"Don't worry," he said. "I will let you use my jacket, so you don't get your hair wet."

"I used to play in the rain all the time when I was a little girl. I'm not worried about my hair. It's just these shoes. I hope I don't fall down! Wait a minute..." Peggy took her shoes off and handed them to Lee. Then, she took his jacket from him and put it over her head. "Are you ready?" she asked.

Lee smiled and laughed. "I've never been readier in my whole life," he said.

"Then here we go!" Peggy said, leading the way out.

They ran across the street to the diner, jumping over puddles and laughing. By the time they got inside, their clothes were wet and limp.

"Please, come in and have a seat wherever you like," a waitress said.

The diner had booths on one side, a long counter with stools on the other side, and a vintage jukebox along the back wall. Peggy and Lee chose a booth near the middle. The jukebox had just started playing "Stand by Me."

They looked across the table at one another and then began to laugh. "I didn't figure our first date would start off like this," Lee said. Soon after, the waitress came over with some menus.

"Hello, my name is Ellen," she said. "What can I start you guys off with to drink? The coffee is great, if you don't plan on sleeping tonight."

"I'll take a glass of water with lemon," Peggy said with a smile.

"Make that two, please," Lee added.

Once the waitress had gone, Peggy began looking through the menu. Lee tried to do the same, but he could not take his eyes off her. She was beautiful, with crystal blue eyes and long brown hair. He had looked into those eyes before, but tonight they seemed to sparkle. He wondered why someone so beautiful would want to go on a date with him.

"What are you going to order?" Peggy asked, snapping him out of it.

Turning his eyes back to the menu, he hesitated for a moment. "I'm going to get the old-fashioned cheeseburger," he said.

"Funny, I was thinking of getting the same thing," she said, "but with no onions or tomatoes."

The waitress returned with two glasses of water. "You guys decide what you're going to get?" she asked, pulling a pad from her apron and a pen from behind her ear.

"Yes, I'll take the old-fashioned cheeseburger with fries, but no onions or tomatoes, please," Peggy said.

"I'll have the same, but add jalapeños to mine," Lee said.

The waitress returned her pad to her apron and then took their menus. Lee thanked her as she walked away.

"Do you mind if I put a song on the jukebox?" he asked.

"Sure," Peggy said with a smile.

"Is there anything you want to hear?"

"Whatever you like will be fine with me."

As Lee approached the jukebox, he saw that it was actually a modern, digital jukebox with a vintage look. Scrolling through the tracks, he recognized all of the music. He saw a list of songs by The Beatles, Nat King Cole, Richie Valens, and Elvis Presley. Then, he found "Peggy Sue" by Buddy Holly and decided to put it on. He turned and began to dance down the aisle.

Peggy laughed as Lee danced back to her, smiling, his shoulders shrugging to the beat of the song. He looked so dorky, but she knew what a good man he was. She began to list to herself everything she liked about him. He was hard working, compassionate, honest, understanding, caring, genuine, and a great listener—everything she wanted from a man. In that moment, she knew that she had fallen for him. She felt elated, as if she were sitting on a cloud, and she thanked God for bringing him into her life.

Lee returned to his seat. "Do you like this song?" he asked, pointing at the ceiling with his elbows on the table. "I thought you might, since your name is in the song and Buddy Holly is from my hometown."

"I love it," she replied, feeling like a schoolgirl.

Lee reached slowly across the table to take her hands, and she moved her hands to meet his. Holding hands over the table, they locked eyes for what seemed like forever. They sat in silence, as if they were entirely alone. In that moment, there was no music from the jukebox and no dishes rattling in the kitchen. Even the rain seemed to have stopped.

The moment lasted until the waitress returned with their food. "Enjoy!" she said, and then walked away, a smile on her face, as well. It was as if the universe had let everyone in on love's little secret.

Still holding hands, Peggy and Lee said a small prayer to bless the food. Then, they began to enjoy their dinner. As they ate, they made light conversation. They talked about their days, the classes Peggy would take the following semester, and what plans they had for the near future.

When they had finished, Lee paid the bill. Then, they walked slowly through a light drizzle back to the car. As was becoming the norm, Lee opened the door for Peggy and closed it behind her when she was settled.

As Lee walked around to the driver's side, a man in a car pulled up beside them. Lee was unable to distinguish much about him in the darkness and the rain, and he did not give it much thought. Instead, he got into the car and drove Peggy home.

When they pulled up in front of her house, Lee turned off the car. He moved to get out and to open her door, but she suggested they talk for a little while longer. More than happy to spend more time with her, Lee stayed put.

"I had a good time tonight. I really enjoyed your company and our conversation," she said with a smile. Then, she sat quietly, gazing at Lee.

Lee reached slowly for her hand, and she took his hand gently in hers. "Me too," he said softly. "And again, I want to apologize about the other restaurant. I really did make a reservation, and I can't believe they messed it up. I meant for everything to be perfect tonight."

"Don't apologize!" she said. "I loved the diner! And I loved that you played that song for me and made me smile. I had so much fun tonight, even though it was raining. Everything was perfect, especially the gentleman you are with me."

Lee smiled, growing happier with every word she said. Even if the night had not been perfect, she was. In that moment, he leaned over slowly and kissed her. She had not expected it, but she was glad and kissed him back.

Letting go of her hands, he placed his hands gently on her face, caressing her softly as they kissed. Suddenly, a loud clap of thunder made them both jump. They laughed again, and Peggy said that someone might be trying to tell them something. She hugged him, squeezing him tightly, and closed her eyes. She did not want to let him go.

"Oh, I'm sorry," she said after a moment. "I didn't mean to squeeze you so hard. The thunder scared me a little. Maybe I should go inside before it starts raining harder again."

"It's okay," he said sweetly. "I didn't mind at all. Let me open your door for you."

Putting her hand on his, she said, "Please, you don't have to. I can open my door." She leaned over and gave him one more kiss. "Thank you, Lee," she said. "I hope you have a great rest of the night."

She opened her door and walked quickly into the house. Lee noticed that Father O'Connor had left the porch light on for her, and it led him to wonder who loved her more, he or her uncle. Smiling at this thought, he started the car and drove home.

# Chapter 9

After dropping his mother off at work several days later, Lee decided to stop by the bar to see Gil. He wanted to ask him about the boxing match. As Lee took a seat at the bar, Gil set down the glasses he had been drying with a rag and reached out to shake his hand. "What's going on, Lee?" he asked. "Can I get you something?"

"No, thank you. I actually just wanted to ask you about that boxing match," Lee said, pointing to the flyer on the wall behind the bar. "Do you know the people sponsoring it?"

"You're in luck, cowboy. The promoter is right over there," Gil said, pointing to a man at the bar a few stools down from Lee.

Lee got up as Gil called out to the promoter. "Doc! Hey Doc! I got someone who wants to meet you. He's a friend of mine."

Doc turned as Lee approached to introduce himself. "How can I help you?" he asked.

"My name is Lee. Are you the man promoting the amateur boxing match?"

"I am. I'm actually looking for new talent, so anybody who wants to fight can enter. The entry fee is five hundred dollars, but the grand prize is five thousand dollars and a chance to move up in the boxing world. You interested?"

"I've been thinking about it, but I haven't got any experience in the ring," Lee said, shifting his feet.

"Son, this is an amateur boxing match. You really don't need experience. All you need is the guts to get in the ring. You're not from Southey, now, are ya?" Doc asked, taking a drink from his bottle of beer.

"He's not from Southey," said a voice that Lee could tell belonged to a local.

He turned to see who had interrupted. When he had, he thought the man may have been the man who drove by him and Peggy on their date. He could not be sure, though.

Doc turned around, too. "What's going on, Mark? Do you know this guy?" he asked, gesturing towards Lee.

"No, but I know he took my ex-girlfriend out to eat the other night," Mark said in his heavy Boston accent. He stepped forward so that his face was just inches away from Lee's. His expression was pure hatred, as if Lee had betrayed him in the worst way.

Lee inched closer to Mark, not wanting to suggest that he would back down. "What are you talking about, man?" he said.

"Peggy."

Lee's face grew angrier. "You said 'ex.' That means she isn't your concern anymore. But she is mine."

Doc got between them. "Alright, guys, chill out," he said. "Let's all have a drink on me! Gil, a round of beers for me and my friends, please."

"Thank you, but I'm going to pass," Lee said, shaking Doc's hand and turning to leave.

"Give me a call if you want to sign up for the match," Doc said. "Here's my card."

"You didn't tell him, Doc?" Mark asked.

"Tell me what?" Lee asked, looking first at Mark and then at Doc.

"If you enter the match," Mark said, taking a swig of his beer, "and if you move up, you will be fighting me!"

Without a word, Lee turned and walked out of the bar.

✝

He drove home with mixed emotions, including frustration. Pulling up in his mother's car, he saw Peggy sitting on the front steps.

She smiled and stood up when she saw him arrive, but then she saw him slam the car door. "What's wrong, Lee? What happened?" she asked as he walked towards her. "Why do you look upset?"

Lee remained silent until he had sat down on the porch. Then, he told Peggy what had happened.

"After I dropped off my mother at work, I decided to stop at the pub to visit Gil. I wanted to find out if he knew anything about the amateur boxing match in October. He told me that the guy promoting the fight was sitting just a couple of stools down from me."

"What did the promoter say?" Peggy asked.

"Well, I introduced myself and asked about the fight, aaand...."

Peggy listened in anticipation; her eyes wide.

"I ran into your ex-boyfriend, Mark."

"What?!"

"Yeah. It gets better. If I fight, I'll be fighting him because no one else has registered in his weight class."

"You're not really considering fighting him," Peggy said.

"Of course not, but I wonder why he was so angry that I took you out to dinner."

"Maybe it's because I never let him take me out to dinner, or maybe he can't stand me being seen with someone so handsome," Peggy said, leaning forward and kissing him on the lips. Then, she changed the subject. "The reason I came by is that my uncle's birthday is on the 21st of September. I know it's still a month away, but I wanted to buy him a gift, and I just don't know what to get him. Do you have any ideas?"

Lee thought for moment, and then he had an idea. "I might know what he'll like," he said, standing up. "How about a new fishing pole?"

Peggy's face broke into a smile. "Perfect!" she said. "Why didn't I think of that! He would love a new fishing pole!" She threw her arms around him. "Thank you," she said.

"No worries!" he said. "Maybe we can go get one tomorrow when I get off work?"

"Sounds great!" Peggy said, excited.

They turned to walk into the house, and Lee held the door for Peggy. As he was about to follow her in, he heard a strange sound. It sounded like a bird, but it was more of a whistle than a chirp. Turning back around, he started scanning the trees for the source of the sound.

"What is it? Is everything okay?" Peggy called from inside.

"Everything's fine," Lee responded, joining her.

The following evening, Lee was cleaning the janitor's room before he went home. As he stowed the buffer and the mop bucket next to his workstation, he noticed the flyer for the boxing match. Feeling frustrated, he picked it up, crushed it into a ball, and threw it into the trashcan by the door. Then, he locked the room and headed home.

The boxing match was still on his mind as he walked down the steps of the College of Education. A man walking up was about to pass him, but then the man stopped and looked at him.

"Hey," he said in a Boston accent, "you're the guy who knocked out those punks who were trying to jump me. My name is Roy." He extended his hand to Lee.

"Lee," Lee said, shaking the man's hand.

"I never got the chance to thank you for saving me from a beating."

"Don't mention it," Lee said, starting back down the concrete steps. Roy followed.

"I take it those guys weren't your friends?" Lee said. "What did you do for them to jump you?"

"They were trying to get me to join their fraternity, but I said I wasn't interested and kind of insulted their intelligence," Roy said. "Hey, I have to get to class, but thanks again. It was nice meeting you." Roy ran up a few steps, but then he stopped suddenly and turned back towards Lee. "Lee!" he called. "In the student union building, there's a flyer promoting an amateur boxing match. You should look into it; you pack a punch! I'll see you around!" Then, Roy turned and walked into the building.

Lee continued on his way to meet Peggy. As he did, he took a moment to listen to what his heart was telling him. Although he was trying to get the boxing match out of his head, it kept inserting itself into his life. He remembered what Father O'Connor had told him. God had a plan for him, he had said, and the Holy Spirit would lead him to it. That sounded right to Lee, and since their conversation, he had been reading the Bible every day and trying to live God's words. The only thing was, he didn't fully understand how it was all supposed to work. He thought about asking Father O'Connor for guidance.

"Lee! Lee!"

Hearing his name shouted in the distance, Lee turned to see Peggy. She was waving to get his attention. He smiled at the sight of her, and his worries faded. Peggy was smiling, too. She walked towards him with her backpack on her back and a few books in her arms.

"How are you, Lee?" she asked, and kissed him softly on the lips.

Lee gave her a hug and then took the books she was carrying. "I'm doing better now that you're here," he said. "How was class?"

"It was okay," she said. "I have an exam next week, but I think I'll do fine. So, do you have any idea where we should go to get my uncle's gift?"

"Yes! I was thinking we should go to Fishing Finatics. It's across the Mystic River, on Main Street. One of my coworkers told me it's a great place to get a fishing rod."

"Oh great!" Peggy said with a smile.

# Chapter 10

They walked across the campus to Peggy's car. When they got there, Lee opened her door and climbed into the driver's seat. Then they drove to their destination.

They arrived at Fishing Finatics a few minutes later, and Lee held the door for Peggy as they walked in. Lee said, "I have a joke for you."

"Oh really?"

"Yes. Why did the fish cross the road?"

Stopping in the middle of the aisle, Peggy turned to him and said, "Why did the fish cross the road? Fish don't have legs, and if one did, why would it get out of the water? That's where fish belong, in the water."

Lee tried to explain the joke, but he admired her persistence in questioning the setup. They went back and forth as they walked through the aisles. Just when Lee was ready to give up on the joke, Peggy caved.

"Lee, tell me why the fish crossed the road."

"Because it got hooked!" Lee said, grabbing a pack of fishhooks from a shelf.

Peggy got the joke, but instead of laughing, she leaned in to stare him directly in the eyes. "Was it..." she paused, "the right hook?" Breaking Lee's gaze, she turned around and walked towards the fishing rods at the back of the store.

As Lee followed her, he wondered why he had a hard time conveying his feelings to her. He knew in his heart he was her knight in shining armor, but he wanted to express his feelings, too. He thought his problem might be he did not know how to say the right words at the right time. He hoped the right time would come soon.

"What about this one?" Peggy asked, pointing to one on the rack.

"Sure!" That's a great one," he said, focusing on the task at hand. He removed the rod gently from the rack so they could get a closer look. "He will love this one," he said.

They decided they had found the right fishing rod, and Lee bought it. Then, he and Peggy drove back to his mother's house.

✝

The next morning, Lee took out his Bible before going to work. He had made a promise to God to strengthen his faith by reading a passage from scripture every day, and he hoped it would also help him to discover where his life should lead. He opened the Bible to Proverbs and scrolled with his finger until the word "trust" caught his eye. The passage was Proverbs 3:5-6, and it said, "Trust in the Lord with all your heart and lean not on your own understanding; in all your ways submit to him, and he will make your paths straight."

Closing the Bible, Lee said a prayer for the day. It made him feel like a new man. Peggy and Father O'Connor had helped him to strengthen his faith, and for that he felt extremely grateful. He hoped he could repay them someday, and he was waiting for the perfect time. As he returned the Bible to his drawer, he heard the same strange chirping he had the day before. Outside his window, he saw the blue jay in the tree. He walked to the window and watched it until it flew away. He wondered why it had been following him. Was it trying to tell him something? Did it symbolize something? He got dressed and went for his morning run. While he had always run on Sundays, he had begun running two miles every morning before work. He did not know whether he would enter the boxing match, but if he did, he wanted to be in shape.

✝

Several weeks later, it was the morning of Father O'Connor's birthday. Peggy and Lee had told him earlier that week they would make him a special dinner. He had left to run a few errands, but he had left a note for Peggy letting her know he could not wait for his dinner.

Peggy had already cleaned the house, and she was decorating the living room and kitchen. Father O'Connor had been talking recently about someday visiting home, so the party was going to have an Irish theme. She had festooned the entire house with green and white streamers and had inflated white balloons to match.

After a few hours, Lee arrived to help Peggy get groceries and make dinner. She came out the front door and locked it behind her. By the time she had reached the car, Lee had got out and opened her door for her. "Thank you, Lee. You're such a gentleman," she said, glowing.

"You're welcome," he replied, shutting the door behind her. "How about we go to Quincy Market?" he asked.

"Yes!" Peggy said excitedly. "I've wanted to go there ever since I moved here. I heard they have fresh produce! I'm so excited for tonight's dinner, and I'm glad you're going to be a part of it."

"Me too," he replied. "Thanks for inviting me, and I truly hope your uncle loves his birthday dinner."

"He will," she said, "especially his birthday gift." At that, they exchanged a glance and smiled.

Peggy's face lit up when they arrived at Quincey Market, and she explained to Lee they had similar markets back home in Ireland. It felt special to Lee to be there with her, and for the first time he saw them as a real couple. She was wearing black skinny jeans, black boots without heels, and an off-white cashmere sweater that complemented her figure. What he loved most about her was her smile, he thought. It made him feel like nothing else mattered. He also loved their long conversations and her Irish accent. He would sometimes try to mimic it, and this made her laugh because she never knew what accent would come out of him, but it was rarely Irish.

Peggy felt the same way about Lee. He had continued to open up to her as they had spent time together, and she believed his renewed faith in God had played a major part in his change. She had not told him, but she prayed for him every night.

"Are you hungry?" she asked.

"Yes," he replied, "the smells from these stands are making me really hungry. How about pizza?" he asked, nodding towards a pizzeria.

"Sounds good to me," she said.

As they stood at the counter to read the menu, Peggy reached out to hold Lee's hand. He gazed into her eyes. Neither spoke, but if they had shared their thoughts, they both would have said, "Don't let go of my heart because it's yours to have."

"What will it be?" asked the man behind the register in an Italian accent. "We'll take two slices of your best oven-baked pepperoni," Lee said, as Peggy looked at the other pizzas through the glass countertop. Lee paid for the pizzas and for two fountain drinks.

"There are two seats over there. I'll go save them for us," Peggy said, walking over to a countertop table.

"Great," Lee said. "What do you want to drink?"

"Iced tea," she replied.

Lee filled their drinks and, balancing their pizza on top, walked over to join Peggy. As they enjoyed their pizza, they watched tourists darting about outside the window.

"I was going to tell you a pizza joke," Lee said, "but..."

Peggy took a bite of her pizza.

"Never mind. It's too cheesy," he finished.

Peggy laughed through her pizza, leaning over the counter and trying to keep from spitting it out. Watching her, Lee laughed as well. Then, he leaned over, put his arms around her, and kissed her on the head.

When they had finished their pizza, they strolled through the market. Seeing a sign for fresh produce, Peggy suggested that they head outside to the farmers' market. Lee held the door for her, and he saw her smile as she passed him. The courtyard was crowded with people—tourists from all over the world as well as Bostonians buying their produce. The stalls overflowed with fruits and vegetables of every kind.

The weather was perfect for a walk, and Lee held Peggy's hand as they strolled. She told him how excited she was to make her uncle his favorite dish, Colcannon, a traditional Irish dish of mashed potatoes and kale or, less often, cabbage. So, they found fresh potatoes, kale, and spring onions.

As they were leaving, Lee eyed the contents of the bags he was carrying and said, "Father O'Connor is going to love that you're making Colcannon, especially from scratch and with fresh ingredients. Did you make it the night I came over for dinner or did your uncle?"

Peggy was not listening. Her eyes were locked on a man approaching them. "Oh, great. The last person I wanted to see," she said, as Lee looked up. "Just ignore him."

# Chapter 11

Lee recognized Mark, Peggy's ex-boyfriend, who stopped in front of them and extended his hand as if to stop them in place. "What do we have here?" he said, looking first at Lee and then at Peggy. "Hi Peggy."

"What do you want, Mark?" Peggy asked, glaring.

"I don't want anything, except to know why your boyfriend is scared to get in the ring with me."

"I'm not scared," Lee said, getting in Mark's face.

Noticing how intense the situation was getting, Peggy put herself between the two and faced Lee. "Don't worry about him! Can we please go?" she asked.

"Yeah, you should go back where you came from, coward!" Mark said.

"Please ignore him. Lee, can we please go?" Peggy asked.

As Lee and Mark finished a long stare-down, Peggy was finally able to lead Lee away by the hand. As they left, Mark gave Lee a little grin and a wink and went on his way.

Lee sat in silence on the drive home to Peggy's. Peggy knew what was bothering him, but she stayed quiet, too. She wanted to avoid adding to his frustration. As they pulled into the driveway, both began their apologies at the same time.

"There's no need to apologize, Peggy," Lee said. "You didn't do anything wrong. He was the one who was trying to get under my skin. I want to apologize for not listening to you the first time. I should have walked away that instant." Lee's face was sincere as he held Peggy's hand. "Oh, no worries. I'm just glad you didn't knock his teeth out," Peggy said with a smile.

"And if I had?"

"Well then, we would be having two parties today, my uncle's and the Boston Teeth Party!" Peggy said, laughing. "Now, let's go inside. You can help me cook." She leaned over to kiss Lee on the lips. Peggy always had a special way of putting a smile on Lee's face.

As they got out of the car and walked inside, Lee continued smiling. Peggy had a cute sense of humor, he thought, but also some tough Irish blood.

✝

Lee helped Peggy make dinner, and then they began setting the table. Although Lee had a smile on his face, Peggy knew the incident with Mark was still bothering him. She walked around the table to him and slowly put her hands on his face, looking him in the eyes. "Lee," she said, "please don't let him get to you. We just need to pray about it." Then, moving her body closer to his, she said, "I know you're an amazing man, and God knows what an incredible life He has in store for you."

"I hope you're a part of it," he replied, gazing into her eyes.

"Me too," Peggy said, and then whispering to him, "I hear something." She walked quickly to the living room window and peeked through the blinds. Outside, she saw her uncle conversing with the priest who had dropped him off. Running back into the kitchen, she said, "It's Uncle! He's about to come in!"

"But sweetie, he knows about his dinner," Lee said, motioning towards the table with a smile.

"I know, silly, but I still want to surprise him when he walks in."

Her beautiful smile showed her excitement, and as it always did, it brought him peace. She had turned off the lights, but a little trickled in through the kitchen windows. Hiding in the dark, they heard the front door open and close. Then, they heard Father O'Connor's footsteps as he made his way to the kitchen. He reached for the switch and flicked on the lights.

"Surprise!" they shouted.

His smile revealed that he was elated by the food, the decorations, and most importantly, the hug Peggy and Lee gave him. "Oh, thank you both," he said. "You guys shouldn't have done all this. It's too much for an old man like me."

"Not at all, Uncle," Peggy said.

"You deserve more," Lee said.

"All I need is right here," he said, with a smile that lit up the room.

"Shall we eat?" Peggy asked.

"The food smells so good! You outdid yourself, Peggy," he replied.

"Oh, I had help from Lee," she said, looking happily at Lee. As Lee and her uncle sat down, she poured tea into their glasses. Then, she sat down herself.

"Does anyone want to say a prayer to bless the food?" Father O'Connor asked.

"I hope you all don't mind, but I would love to," Peggy said. They bowed their heads as Peggy began to pray.

"Heavenly Father, we thank you for bringing us around this table for the special meal you have provided for us. Lord, I pray you would also nourish our hearts and refresh our souls. Lord, I also pray we may be mindful of the needs of others. We give you all of the honor and all of the glory. In your name we pray every day. Amen."

"Amen," said Lee and Father O'Connor when she had finished.

Then, turning to Peggy, Father O'Connor said, "I spoke to your father and mother today. They called me earlier to wish me happy birthday."

"Oh really? That was so nice of them," Peggy said as she passed the dish of colcannon to Lee.

"They wanted me to give you the good news today," Father O'Connor continued.

Lee and Peggy shared a look of surprise.

"What's the good news, Uncle?" Peggy asked.

"They are coming next month to visit," he said with a smile.

"Oh, I can't wait to see Mom and Dad!" Peggy said excitedly, looking at Lee.

Lee was happy for her, and he tried to show it. However, he could not stop thinking about the incident with Mark and about the upcoming boxing match. This made him feel out of place. Father O'Connor soon noticed Lee's distance and asked how his day had been.

Lee demurred at first, not wanting to spoil Father O'Connor's birthday dinner by talking about himself. Father O'Connor was persistent, however, and eventually asked, "Is everything alright, son?"

Peggy looked towards Lee, wondering whether he was going to mention what had happened at the market.

"Yes, everything is okay, Father," Lee said, continuing to eat.

To prevent an awkward moment, Peggy interjected. "Well," she said to Father O'Connor, "I say we light the candles on your birthday cake as soon as we finish dinner so you can make a wish."

"Oh, Peggy," Father O'Connor said, "in that case, I might have to stop eating right now to leave room for dessert."

"I'll get the cake. Excuse me," Lee said, getting up and walking to the counter. He picked up the lighter that had been placed beside the cake and used it to light the candles. One of the candles was shaped like the number eight, and the other was shaped like the number zero. Then, he picked up the cake and began walking with it towards the table.

As he approached, Peggy began recording the scene on her phone. They sang "Happy Birthday," and then Father O'Connor blew out the candles.

"Did you make a wish?" Lee asked.

"I did," Father O'Connor replied with a smile. Peggy began to cut the cake, and Lee went back to the counter for silverware and paper plates. "Lee," Father O'Connor said, "a little bird told me you've been running every morning before work. Does that have anything to do with the boxing match coming up?"

Lee wondered for a moment whether Peggy had said something, but he knew her better than to believe she had. She had been loyal to him, and he knew he could trust her with anything.

"I have eyes and ears," Father O'Connor said, as if he had been reading Lee's thoughts.

Recognizing the issue was not going to go away and he was with two people to whom he could tell anything, Lee relented. He swallowed the lump in his throat and described his situation. He said his main reason for wanting to enter the match was to win money for a car.

When he had finished, Father O'Connor offered words of wisdom and lessons from scripture. Lee listened and was grateful, but this time, he offered his own wisdom and lessons. "To win a battle of any kind," he said, "you must first believe in your mission, and your mission is to believe you can do anything, especially with the Lord beside you. In Deuteronomy, the Bible says, 'when you are approaching the battle, the priest shall come near and speak to the people.'"

Lee paused. "Isn't it weird I'm talking to you about this?" he said with a confused look on his face. As he did, he wondered why God had put him in the situation.

Tears of gratitude filled Father O'Connor's eyes as he realized Lee was really learning his scripture. He said, "Deuteronomy 31:6 also says 'be strong and courageous, do not be afraid or tremble at them, for the Lord your God is the one who goes with you. He will not fail you or forsake you.'"

"I'm very sorry, Father O'Connor," Lee replied. "I really didn't mean to bother you with my worries, especially on your birthday."

Lee really did feel bad, but he also felt relief at having spoken his mind to people who really cared about him.

Recognizing Lee's vulnerability, Peggy reached across the table for his hand. She knew it had been hard for him to vent to Father O'Connor in front of her. They sat in silence for a while, and then Peggy stood and began collecting the dishes. Lee cut himself another slice of cake. Before he could take a bite, however, Father O'Connor reached across the table and took his plate. "Do you think another slice of cake is what you need to train for the match?" he asked.

"Uncle, I don't think Lee's going to enter," Peggy said, clearing the table.

"She's right," Lee said. "And anyway, I really don't know anything about boxing in a ring."

"No," Father O'Connor replied, "but you have a good hook, and that's a good start. You can learn the rest in training."

"Training? Who's going to train me? I don't have the money to pay for a trainer."

"I'm not asking for money," Father O'Connor said, his Irish accent coming through. "I'm asking for determination."

Peggy stopped cleaning and looked between Lee and her uncle.

"What are you saying, Father?" Lee asked.

"Son, what I'm trying to say is I'm an old Irish man and I'm brittle, but if you need a trainer, I wouldn't mind at all. But I do have two conditions. First, you must promise to believe in yourself. Second, you must promise not to punch me."

Everyone laughed.

"I promise!" Lee said, his heart filled with joy.

Peggy hugged Lee and then circled the table to hug Father O'Connor.

"This is the best gift I could have received," Lee said.

"Speaking of gifts," Peggy said, "I have to go get your gift, Uncle. Just wait here."

As Peggy went upstairs to her room, Lee thanked Father O'Connor again for everything he had done for him. He told him he was right about God having a plan for him and that meeting him was part of it. He wished there were some way for him to truly show his appreciation, but he still had not thought of one.

"Training starts at seven o'clock in the morning," Father O'Connor said.

"Close your eyes, Uncle!" Peggy said, coming downstairs.

Father O'Connor closed his eyes.

"Okay, open them!" she said.

When he did, Peggy handed him the fishing rod.

"This is exactly what I needed!" he said, elated both with his gift and to be spending his birthday with Peggy and Lee. "I can't wait to go fishing! Now, all I need to catch the big one, is the right hook!"

Soon after, Father O'Connor said it was getting late for him and said goodnight to Peggy and Lee. Lee made sure to thank him again, and then he helped Peggy to clean the kitchen. When the kitchen was clean, they also decided to call it a night, and Peggy walked him out. Taking her hands in his, he said, "Thank you for being you, for supporting me, for caring for me, and for letting me be a part of your life. I thank God for sending me an angel, and I truly believe he did." Then, he leaned close and gazed into her eyes for a few seconds and slowly said, "You calm my soul." Afterwards he softly and gently kissed her lips.

# Chapter 12

The following morning, Lee was awakened by a beautiful chirping. Getting out of bed, he walked towards the window and once again saw the blue jay outside on the branch. He could not give much thought to the continued appearance of the bird, however, because today was his first day of training. After reading a passage from the Bible and saying a prayer, Lee got dressed and headed out on his morning run. This time, he ran to Father O'Connor's house. When he arrived, he found a note on the door that read, "Your training starts now. Run to the lake. That's where I'll be."

By the time Lee got to the lake, he felt slightly exhausted. He took a minute to admire the scenery before meeting Father O'Connor. He could not quite grasp what it was, but something felt special about that lake.

"How's the fishing rod working for you?" he asked, walking up to Father O'Connor.

"Oh, it's a beauty to fish with," Father O'Connor replied. "I've been getting bites here and there, but I haven't caught anything yet. How was your run?"

"It was okay," Lee said.

Father O'Connor nodded. "There are some things we should discuss before your training starts," he said. "First, do you have friends who could help you with the things I no longer can because of my age? You will need two guys, and they must be as serious about your training as you are. Second, I want you to know that the most important thing in boxing is your physical and mental agility.

Today, we will be focusing on your physical agility. Your heart is the strongest muscle in your body, and we need to get it healthy. So, you will be drinking lots of water and doing lots of running."

"So, Father," Lee said, "what do you have planned for me today?"

"Well, Lee, if you don't mind, please grab that tackle box," Father O'Connor said. Then, he stood up, grabbed his folding chair, and began walking towards his truck. Lee grabbed the tackle box and followed. "When we get to my truck," Father O'Connor said, "I want you to do fifty push-ups. Then, we will continue at my house."

When they got to the truck, Father O'Connor put his chair and fishing pole in the back. Lee threw in the tackle box, and then he began his push-ups. Before he could finish, Father O'Connor got in the truck and drove off. Getting up quickly, Lee caught a glimpse of him in the rearview mirror. He was smiling with his hands in the air. Lee got the feeling that his training was not going to be easy.

✝

On Friday night of the following week, Peggy and Lee surprised Lee's mother at work. Lee had not yet mentioned the boxing match to her, and he was afraid she might not take it well. He was also excited for Peggy to meet her.

Peggy was excited, too. Lee talked a lot about his mother, but Peggy had not had a chance to meet her because of her work schedule. As they waited for her in the lobby, Lee got the same weird feeling he always got at hospitals. Describing the feeling to Peggy, he told her he had lost his grandmother when he was eight years old. So many of his family members had cried, he remembered, especially his mother. That was how he had known that she had been hurt by the loss. Even though he had been young, Lee explained, he had begun to understand that death is a part of life.

A few moments later, Lee's mother walked into the lobby. Lee greeted her with a hug. "Mom, I want to introduce you to Peggy," he said. "Peggy, this is my mother, Sandra."

Peggy reached out to shake Sandra's hand, but Sandra said, "I have to hug you, sweetie, because I'm pretty sure you're responsible for the happiness I see in my son these days."

Peggy hugged her back. "Thank you," she said, "but I don't want to take all the credit. I believe God had a lot to do with it."

"Lee, I already love her," Sandra said, smiling at Peggy.

"Mom, I have some news for you," Lee said, looking down.

"What's wrong?" she asked quickly, lowering herself into a chair. Lee and Peggy also sat.

"Nothing's wrong, Mom, I just wanted to let you know that I'm going to enter an amateur boxing match. I want you to be there."

"Boxing match?" she said. "But why, Lee?"

"Listen, Mom, it's just an amateur boxing match, and if I win, there's a prize of five thousand dollars."

Touching his face softly with her hands, she said, "I don't want anyone laying their hands on my son's handsome face." At that, Peggy smiled. "Why do you need the money?" she asked. "Please, tell me it's not to buy a car."

"Yes, Mother. I've been using your car for too long, and it's time for me to get my own transportation."

"I guess that explains why you've been getting up to run when I've been getting home from work, but, Lee, you don't know anything about boxing."

Hugging her, he said, "Mom, I'm going to be fine. Trust me." He paused for a moment, looking at Peggy over his mother's shoulder. Then he said, "I have a great trainer."

Watching Lee with his mother, Peggy thought again how special he was. The three of them visited for a few more minutes before Sandra had to return to work. Before they left, Lee gave his mother the details of the match, including when and where it would be.

✝

Lee's friends arrived from Texas a few days later. Big Hym and Sam had both grown up in Lubbock, and they had known Lee since they were kids. Big Hym was indeed big. But although he had the look of a bodyguard, he had the personality of a teddy bear. Sam had seen some hard times, and they had made him tough. He had spent some time in the ring, but the streets had gotten the better of him. Both had been loyal friends to Lee from the start. They had been family to Lee when his family was rarely around.

Father O'Connor recognized as soon as he met Big Hym and Sam that they were like brothers to Lee, and they joined in his training right away. In addition to running, Lee began training in Father O'Connor's garage.

✝

One morning, Lee, Big Hym, and Sam arrived early and cleaned the garage from top to bottom. When Father O'Connor arrived, the change brought him to tears. Inspecting his medals, trophies, and pictures, which were now free of dust, Father O'Connor relived aloud some of the moments they represented. It made him feel young, and he put that energy into Lee's training.

"Lee," he said, "today's training will be all about intensity. I want you to feel like you're in the ring at all times, especially when you hit the bag. Every time you throw a punch, you have to be ready to get punched! It's not about getting angry or swinging hard at your opponent; it's about being consistent with every punch and controlling your breathing throughout."

Taking Father O'Connor's words to heart, Lee tried hard to stay focused, but it was difficult to focus on the training and not the fight. As the day progressed, however, he began to understand he was surrounded by people who loved him. This cleared his head. He wanted to do it for Father O'Connor, the person who had helped him to see his life differently. Father O'Connor had not seen a fighter in him. Instead, he had planted a seed and let the Holy Spirit do the rest. Since Lee had returned to his Bible, he had learned God uses people to help people. Recognizing this, he wanted to do for Father O'Connor what Father O'Connor had done for him. He figured the best way to do that would be to do his best in the ring.

As Lee trained, Father O'Connor coached him. "Focus, Lee!" he said. "Focus on your stance. Remember, if you are throwing with your right, your left foot should be in front. If you are throwing with you left, your right foot should be in front; that's called fighting 'southpaw.'" As he spoke, his Irish accent came out. "Now, keep your elbows close to your ribs after you throw a punch. Jab! Jab! Keep moving around the bag, Lee. Don't forget to breathe. When you're working on a hook, it will be different than throwing a jab or a cross. The power behind your hook will come from your legs, hips, and especially your upper body. It takes a lot of energy, so you have to be accurate with your punches."

# Chapter 13

During Lee's training, Peggy would often make quick snacks for everyone. One day, however, Big Hym and Sam decided to barbeque in the backyard. They grilled a whole brisket, and they made corn on the cob, hot links, and Texas Jalapeño Poppers. Peggy and Father O'Connor enjoyed the company, and they were both happy to see Lee having a good time. Father O'Connor had excused himself and gone inside, and Lee was sitting next to Peggy and having a drink of water. As he drank, he spied the blue jay in a nearby tree. He again wondered why he kept seeing it, but this time he remembered Jack had drawn blue jays all the time. He did not know if this blue jay was a connection to Jack's blue jays or if there was any connection at all, but the bird was appearing more often these days.

"Who's ready for some barbeque?" Big Hym called, taking the brisket off the grill. This snapped Lee out of his daydream, and he, Peggy, and Sam followed Big Hym inside.

While Lee had been daydreaming, Father O'Connor had been on the telephone, inviting an old friend to the boxing match. He had hung up just before they came in.

"Uncle?" Peggy called.

"I'm coming," he replied.

"Is everything alright?"

"Yes, Peggy, everything is alright. Good! Dinner is ready."

They all sat at the kitchen table and enjoyed Big Hym's and Sam's Texas barbeque. Lee felt like he was back home, and they all shared stories. Big Hym and Sam reminisced about the old days, when all of them were young and used to get into trouble. Then, Father O'Connor told a story. As soon as he began, Lee sensed something different in his voice. The others must have, too, because everyone fell silent and listened intently.

"There was a man from Sweden," the story began. "His name was Alfred, and he grew up curious about life. As an adult, he became a chemist, an engineer, and an inventor, and he joined the family business of making explosives. He eventually invented and patented the explosive that we call 'dynamite.' He made millions. Some used dynamite for good, while others used it for evil. When Alfred's brother passed away, Alfred found his obituary in the local newspaper. But there had been a mistake. Instead of his brother's obituary, the newspaper had accidentally published Alfred's own. It said awful things about him, including that he had sold dynamite with the intention of killing people. Reading this made Alfred reflect on who he really was. Reaching the conclusion that what the obituary had said was true, he decided to turn his life around. He created a scholarship for students who demonstrated outstanding achievement in chemistry, medicine, physics, and humanitarianism. Society recognized the good he had done. After his good contribution, the most prestigious prize in the world was named after him: The Nobel Peace Prize."

Pausing for a moment, Father O'Connor finished his story by quoting scripture. "Isaiah 43:18 says, 'forget the former things; do not dwell on the past.'"

Having finished, Father O'Connor got up, thanked Big Hym and Sam for the barbeque, and said goodnight. Leaving the room, he paused in the doorway. Turning his head, he said, "God hates sin, but God loves the sinner." Big Hym and Sam would never forget that moment, and they all sat in silence for what seemed like a long time. Then, they helped Peggy put away the leftovers. As they did, they told her how great her uncle was and how lucky they had been to have heard the incredible story he shared. Lee was not surprised, having already known how wise Father O'Connor was, but he felt blessed by their friendship. When the kitchen was in order, they all said goodbye to Peggy and drove back to Lee's mother's house, where they were all staying.

When Lee awoke early the next morning, he reached into the drawer of his nightstand, took out his Bible, and began reading a passage from scripture aloud. As he read, he heard Big Hym's and Sam's alarm going off downstairs, where they had each claimed a couch. They heard him speaking upstairs, and they soon came up to check on him. He finished reading just as they walked in.

"What were you doing?" Sam asked.

"Thinking about my future," Lee replied.

"I hope your future has running in it, because it's time to start," Big Hym said.

"Meet me at Father O'Connor's house," Lee said. "I'm going to run to the lake, and then I'll head that way."

✝

When he got to the lake, like usual Lee rested for a minute to catch his breath and take in the scenery, which was so peaceful and beautiful it could have been painted on canvas. The cherry blossom trees and low bushes beside the bench were reflected flawlessly in the placid water until a tiny gust of wind sent ripples through them. It was as if nature was clearing its canvas to make room for a fresh work of art. Lee had caught his breath and was getting ready to resume running when he heard a honk. Turning, he saw Father O'Connor waving to him from his truck, and he knew the time had come to begin his daily training.

When they got back to the garage, Lee began sparring with Sam. Knowing the match was only a week away, he stayed focused. "Work the body!" Father O'Connor shouted. "Don't forget to breathe every time you swing!" After a few hours, Lee was lighter on his feet, and his punches were getting much faster. Father

O'Connor looked on approvingly, as if he felt Lee was ready for his match.

✝

Meanwhile, that night, Peggy picked Lee up at home to take him on a date. When she knocked on the door, he answered.

"Hi Peggy, are you ready?" he asked.

"Yes, but I need you to do me a favor."

"Sure, what is it?" he said, kissing her.

"I need you to go back inside and find me something I can blindfold you with, please," she said, smiling.

"Okay..." Lee said, as if she was losing her mind. Then, he went to find a blindfold. When he returned, he handed her a white bandana. She motioned for him to turn around. He did, allowing himself to be blindfolded.

"I'm doing this because I don't want you to know where I'm taking you to dinner," she explained in her Irish accent.

"But I always open the door for you, sweetie," he said. "Can you guide me to the driver's side so I can? Then, I will feel my way around to my side." She agreed, and like a gentleman, he opened her door. As he did, Peggy marveled at the huge effects his simple gestures had on her.

When they arrived at the restaurant, Peggy reached for a gift that she had hidden in the back seat. "We're here," she said, "but don't take off your blindfold. I'm going to open your door for you."

Lee felt a little anxious not knowing where he was, but he knew he was safe in Peggy's hands. She helped him out of the car and then walked him through the door of the restaurant. "We're here!" she said beside him.

"Can I take my blindfold off?" he asked.

"Yes," she said.

As soon as he had uncovered his eyes, he lifted Peggy in a hug and kissed her lips. She had taken him to the diner where they had eaten on their first date. On the table they had shared that night, he saw a present. She took his hands in hers and led him towards their booth as "My Girl" began playing on the jukebox. Several people were eating in the restaurant as well.

"Whose gift is that?" Lee asked, as Peggy moved the gift to one side.

"It's yours, but I don't want you to open it until we finish eating."

They sat down and a waitress came to their table. "Welcome, my name is Ellen," she said, looking between them as if she remembered their faces. "What can I start you guys off with to drink?"

"Two glasses of water with lemon," Peggy said, clearly comfortable ordering for Lee.

He looked at her and smiled, remembering their first date. He began singing along to "My Girl" and reached across the table to take her hands.

The waitress returned with their waters. "You guys ready to order, or do you need a minute?" she asked.

"We need a minute, please," Peggy said. Lee was looking over the menu, and as he did, Peggy reflected on how lucky she was to have a boyfriend as kind and a real gentleman as he had been from the start.

"Do you know what you're going to order?" Lee asked.

"I think I'm going to get the old-fashioned cheeseburger—"

"With no onions or tomatoes," Lee said, finishing her sentence.

"Yes," she said, smiling at him. Lee orders the same meal as Peggy.

When the waitress had taken their orders, they both shared how happy they were to be with each other. Peggy told Lee what a great person he had become and how there had been a huge change in his personality since they had first met. Lee responded by thanking her for being the amazing person she was and for having faith in him on his new journey. Peggy was elated by the things Lee was saying to her and knew she was head over heels for him, but she doubted her ability to express herself. She thought maybe this was not the time or the place to do so.

Their food arrived, and their conversation continued as they ate.

"How do you feel your training is going?" she asked.

"I'm loving it every day, thanks to your uncle," he said. "He's been so great with me."

"I'm glad you're happy."

"But I'm happier when I'm with you," he said, smiling at her.

Peggy moved their plates aside and put his present in the center of the table. "Lee," she said, "I want to tell you my feelings for you have grown deeper as we have spent time together. There are wonderful things about you that make me want to continue getting to know you. You're ambitious now, and it's like clay being sculpted into a masterpiece. It warms my heart. You inspire me to better myself every day." As she said this, she began to tear up. "You calm my soul," she said.

Leaning over the table, Lee kissed her softly and caressed the back of her neck with his fingers. Then, he sat back and held her hands.

Soon after, the waitress brought the check and cleared the table. "Thank you, guys. Come back soon," she said.

"Okay, now I want you to open your gift, sweetie," Peggy said.

Lee untied the beautiful bow and then tore open the wrapping paper. As he did, Peggy smiled in anticipation. When he had removed enough of the paper, his face lit up with excitement and joy. Folded in the box were new boxing shorts. Lifting them out, he saw that they were white with a red stripe down both sides. Then, he saw a small blue jay embroidered in the bottom corner of the right side. As he ran his fingers gently over the bird, the emotion was plain in his face.

"I remembered you telling me that when you were young, your friend Jack used to draw blue jays," Peggy said. "So, I figured maybe this one would bring you luck."

Lee was speechless for a moment, unable to express the contents of his heart. Then, he said, "Thank you, Peggy. You are so kind and thoughtful. I can't believe you did this for me. I will never forget this day." His heart still full of emotion, he gazed into her beautiful blue eyes and said, "I love you." Then, he leaned over the table and kissed her passionately on the lips.

# Chapter 14

Even though less than a week remained until Lee's boxing match, Father O'Connor continued to teach at the University once a week. His class was just about to end, and he concluded with a reading from Hebrews 10: 24-25, "And let us consider how we may spur one another on towards love and good deeds, not giving up meeting together, as some are in the habit of doing, but encouraging one another—and all the more as you see the day approaching."

"God hates sin, but God loves the sinner!" he said. Then, his students joined him in saying "Amen!"

As the other students left, Peggy returned her books to her backpack. Father O'Connor put his Bible in his briefcase, and he told her that he would be waiting for her in the hallway. A moment later, she threw her backpack over her shoulder and walked out the door.

When she stepped into the hallway, her parents were waiting for her. With a gasp, she dropped her backpack on the floor and hugged them. She had known they were planning to visit from Ireland, but she had not expected them until the following week. "I've missed you both so much!" she said. "And Uncle has, too!"

Father O'Connor smiled at Peggy.

"We missed you, too, Peggy Grace," her father said in Irish accent even thicker than her own. Her father had called her Peggy Grace since she was a baby. Her mother hugged her tightly for a moment and then kissed her on her cheek.

"I'm glad you're here. I want to introduce you to someone," she said excitedly.

After greeting one another for a few more moments, they walked together down the hallway and out of the building.

"Your uncle has informed us you met a young man," her mother said, wrapping her arm around her.

"I have. His name is Lee, and I believe he's a good person."

"Your uncle thinks the same," her mother replied. Behind them, Father O'Connor and Peggy's father were having their own conversation.

When they arrived at the College of Education, Lee was just exiting the building.

"Lee!" Peggy called, waving to him.

"Hi, Peggy," he said, giving her a hug.

"I want to introduce you to my mom, Saoirse, and my dad, Sean," she said.

"It's a pleasure meeting y'all," Lee said, shaking their hands. "Hello, Father O'Connor," he added.

Peggy told him that since he and Father O'Connor still had to train that day, she and her parents would grab a bite to eat and meet up with them later. Then, they said their goodbyes and Peggy and her parents departed. Once they had, Father O'Connor asked Lee to sit with him on a nearby bench.

"Lee, I wanted to talk to you about the match," he said. "I have to say, you've been training really hard and, thanks in part to your friends, I've had a great time working with you."

"Do you think I'm ready, Father?" Lee asked.

"I think you have the skills you will need in the ring, but as to whether you are mentally prepared, only you can know that."

Lee sat in silence, contemplating the question.

"I hope you don't mind, but I have a good friend who might come to watch you."

"I don't mind at all. I just hope I don't let you down."

"That's not possible," Father O'Connor said. "I'm proud of you, Lee, and I know Peggy is, too."

✝

The day before the big fight, Peggy took her parents sightseeing while Lee, Father O'Connor, Big Hym and Sam did some last-minute training. On the wall of the garage, Lee noticed a new picture, one of him in his boxing stance with Father O'Connor beside him. Peggy had taken it one day when they were training in the backyard. As Lee looked at the picture, he noticed something in the tree behind him and Father O'Connor. He started to lean closer to see what it was.

"Let's get to work!" Father O'Connor said, startling him.

"Yes, Father," he said, putting down the picture. He reached for his boxing gloves, but they were nowhere to be found.

"Can you open that box for me, please?" Father O'Connor asked.

As Lee picked up and opened the box, he asked, "Have y'all seen my..."

Before he could finish his sentence, he realized that the box contained a new pair of red boxing gloves. He smiled, and his heart was filled with emotion.

"We all pitched in," Father O'Connor said, gesturing to Sam and Big Hym.

There was a brief moment of silence, and then Big Hym said, "Those boxing gloves aren't going to box themselves."

"Put them on, and let's get to work!" Sam said.

Lee finished his training that day with new energy, confident that he was ready for whatever tomorrow would bring.

✝

When Lee awoke the next morning, he laid in bed for a moment in bed, staring up at the ceiling. Protruding from the wall above him was the nail from which the rosary had hung when he first arrived. Leaning over, he took the Bible and the rosary from his drawer. Then, he sat up, held the rosary in his hands, closed his eyes, and began to pray. When he had finished, he kissed the rosary and hung it from the nail. Then, he read a passage from scripture and returned the Bible to the drawer.

"Lee, breakfast is ready!" his mother shouted from downstairs.

Walking down, he heard his friends conversing at the table.

"Good morning, Lee," his mother said.

"Good morning, Mom. Morning, guys," Lee said, sitting down in front of his plate.

"Morning, brother," Big Hym said. Sam had food in his mouth, but he nodded.

Lee said a small prayer before beginning to eat.

"How do you feel about today?" his mother asked.

"I feel bless," he replied.

"That's good!" she said.

"Hey, Lee, no matter what happens tonight, I just want to say I'm proud of you," Sam said.

"Yeah, me too," Big Hym said. "Moving up here was the best thing for you, and meeting Father O'Connor made a huge impact on your life. It was truly a true blessing."

"Thanks again, guys," Lee said. "Thanks for coming up here. I really don't know how to show you my appreciation."

"There's no need to," Sam said.

"We're family, and since you're my brother, you won't mind if I take your last piece of bacon," Big Hym said, reaching over the table to snatch it from Lee's plate.

Everyone laughed at that, as if they were all kids again.

# Chapter 15

Later that afternoon, Lee's father called him at the house. They generally talked three times a week, but this time his dad wanted to wish him luck and to tell him he wished he could be there. Lee understood why he could not be. His dad's job at the oil field kept him busy most of the time. When Lee hung up the phone, he heard the doorbell ring. Peggy had dropped by to check on him. He loved that about Peggy: she was always concerned with how people were doing. After giving him some last-minute encouragement, she told him she was going to take her parents to the market and then meet him at the gym, where the match was being held. She also told him she would save a seat for his mother. They would all be in the front row, she said, cheering him on. Lee thanked her, and he promised to tell his mother about her seat. They hugged each other goodbye, and then Peggy drove away.

Once she had gone, Lee sat down on the porch steps and reflected on how far he had come since he had first arrived at his mother's house, unsure of where his life would take him. Behind him, he heard the squeak of the screen door opening.

"Are you okay, Son?" his mother asked, sitting beside him.

"I'm okay, Mom," he replied. "I was just admiring your garden." He paused for a moment. Then he said, "Dad still waters the rose bushes you planted back home."

His mother smiled. "He told me he wants to come visit you for Thanksgiving," she said. "He called last week. I believe you were out with Peggy that day."

Lee had noticed his dad always asked about his mother when he called.

"Do you miss him?" he asked her.

She had been looking at her flowers, and her eyes lingered for a moment before she turned and responded. "I do," she said.

Not wanting to pry, Lee left it at that. He was happy his parents had begun to talk more.

His mother stood up and then bent to kiss him on the head.

"Before I forget," Lee said, "Peggy said she is saving you a seat at the match."

"That's sweet of her. I'll be sure to thank her when I see her tonight," she said. Then, she went back inside.

By himself again, Lee looked up through the trees, searching for the blue jay. He was nowhere to be found. After a few minutes, Big Hym joined him. "What time is Father O'Connor picking us up?" he asked.

"Four thirty," he said after a moment, still searching the trees. Then, giving up, he stood and followed Big Hym inside.

When Father O'Connor arrived, they climbed into his truck and headed to the gym. Lee sat shotgun, and Father O'Connor noticed he was cracking his knuckles anxiously. By the time they arrived, however, Lee had known his hard work and training were going to pay off.

✝

In the locker room, Father O'Connor, Big Hym, and Sam helped Lee get ready. Father O'Connor wrapped Lee's left hand with boxing tape, looping it first around his thumb, then around his wrist, then around his palm, and then around his fingers. He repeated the process three times, and then he did the same for Lee's right hand. As he did, he remembered when others had done the same for his hands.

"Boys, can Lee and I have a few minutes alone?" he asked. Once Big Hym and Sam had stepped out into the hallway, he began to talk. "Lee, before I start talking about what you need to do in the ring, there is something I must say. Every morning when you get up, it's important to give thanks to God. We must ask him to guide us through our daily lives. Peggy told me you made a promise to God to read a passage from the Bible every morning. That's good, Lee. When you do that, you allow God into your heart and mind, to guide you with His wisdom and give you knowledge. Young people today are quick to pick up a magazine, watch TV, or lose themselves on their phones, but they are slow to read the Bible, go to church, or maintain a consistent relationship with God. I believe God always walks with you on your journey, so you need never fear any of the challenges He sets before you."

Lee listened attentively as Father O'Connor continued.

"There is one more thing," he said, and then paused for what seemed like a long time. "Lee, when you are confronted by the presence of our lord, Jesus Christ, there is no place to hide. You can't hide, and there is no reason to hide."

Hearing these words, Lee felt the same way he had at the lake when he had first opened up to Father O'Connor. He smiled, again appreciating the power of Father O'Connor's words.

"I'm proud of you, Lee," Father O'Connor said, "and I want to thank you for letting me be a part of this. It has been truly fulfilling, training you."

"Father, you have been a true blessing to me," Lee said. "You had faith in me when I didn't have faith in myself. Thank you for encouraging me to strengthen my faith. I know God put you on my path for that reason, and for that I thank Him." Lee paused, and then he said, "Thank you for being a great friend."

There was a knock at the door, and Father O'Connor got up to open it. It was Peggy.

"Hi, Uncle. Can I come in?" she asked.

"Sure," he replied.

"Hi, Lee, I just wanted to wish you luck and check on how you were feeling," she said, giving him a hug and a kiss.

"I feel great," Lee said. "I just hope I do good out there."

"You will, sweetie."

At that moment, Doc entered with Big Hym, Sam, and Jerry, who Doc introduced as the announcer. Doc reminded Lee of the rules for the fight, including that it would last six rounds. When he had finished, he and Jerry left. Peggy was saying goodbye to Lee when Jerry came back into the room.

"I'm sorry," Jerry said. "There's just one more thing. How do you want me to introduce you, and what music do you want to be playing when you walk out?"

Lee looked at Jerry and then at Peggy. "Peggy," he said, "can you please write my name on a piece of paper and pick out a good song for me?"

"Okay," she said, though her expression was uncertain. Then, she walked out with Jerry.

Big Hym closed the door behind them as they left. Then, Father O'Connor, Big Hym, and Sam began getting Lee warmed up, massaging his shoulders, arms, and neck.

"Lee," Father O'Connor said, "in the first round, I want you to throw some jabs and a few combinations. He will probably do the same. The purpose will be to gauge his reach, so don't waste your energy. Keep moving around the ring and pace yourself. Remember, the most important thing is to control your breathing."

Lee began shadow boxing as he listened.

"In the second round, you'll have chances to hit harder," Father O'Connor continued. "Make sure to protect your head and your body and to move after every hard punch you throw. If you get tired, stay off the ropes and keep moving around. If you stop, you risk showing him you're weakening. After the second round, we can adjust our game plan based on what we have learned about your opponent."

Lee was focused and ready. They could hear Jerry's voice echoing through the gym, thanking the match's sponsors.

"Okay, boys, let's say a quick prayer," Father O'Connor said. They held hands in a circle, and Father O'Connor began. "Heavenly Father, we gather here to give thanks for everything you have given us. We thank you for giving us life, Lord, and I thank you for putting these special young men in my life. I pray you fill their lives with your goodness, and today, Lord, I especially pray you give Lee the strength to do his best, no matter the outcome. I pray he will continue to give you all of the honor and all of the glory. In the name of the Father, the Son, and the Holy Spirit, Amen."

"God hates sin, but God loves the sinner," Lee said.

"Amen," they said together.

They left the locker room and headed down the hallway. When they reached the end, they waited outside the gym for Jerry to introduce Lee. In the distance, near the ring, Lee could see his mother, Peggy, and her parents. He also spotted Gil, the bartender, and Roy, the student he had saved from a beating. He also saw a man in a suit, but he could not see the man's face.

Soon, Jerry announced him. "Our first fighter hails from Lubbock, Texas. Standing at five feet, nine inches and weighing in at one hundred and sixty-five pounds, here is Buddy Lee!"

They all looked at each other.

"Buddy Lee?" Big Hym asked.

Their confusion deepened when Lee's song began to play; it was "Everybody," by Buddy Holly. Lee caught Peggy's eye and shrugged. Peggy did the same and smiled.

Lee began to walk towards the ring with Father O'Conner, Big Hym, and Sam following behind him. He could hear Sam and Big Hym mumbling about the song, but he knew that if he turned to see their faces, he would start laughing and lose his concentration. He kept his eyes forward. When they made it to the ring, Lee shadow boxed to stay loose.

The announcer introduced his opponent. It was Mark who stands the same height and same weight as Lee.

Mark made his way towards the ring, and when he got close, he saw Peggy and blew her a kiss. "I'm going to knock him out and send him back home!" he shouted in his Boston accent.

Peggy did not seem bothered at all. "Stay focused, sweetie!" she yelled to Lee.

When Mark entered the ring, he raised his arms in the air to get the crowd going. They cheered louder and louder.

Soon, the referee summoned Lee and Mark to the center of the ring. Lee's expression was calm as they approached one another, but Mark looked eager to fight and was punching his gloves together. The referee explained he wanted a clean fight and told them to obey the rules. They touched gloves and went to their corners. Father O'Connor put Lee's mouthpiece in and said, "Focus on your jab!"

Then, the bell rang.

In the first round, Lee succeeded in moving around the ring. He threw very few punches, but he landed most of the punches he threw. He tried to block some of Mark's punches, but he realized it was going to be harder than he thought. This was not a street fight, this guy knew what he was doing. He had to focus on what Father O'Connor taught him.

The bell rang to end the first round, and Lee took a seat on the small stool that Sam had lowered into the ring. "You're doing good, Lee," Father O'Connor said, as Big Hym gave him water. "Keep breathing out there and work that jab towards the body."

When the bell rang to start the second round, the crowd got louder. "Pace yourself," Big Hym said. Lee and Mark both began to land jabs. Lee was quick to throw when Mark lowered his gloves, but Mark was experienced and knew how to control his opponents. Feeling some pressure, Lee began throwing combinations to throw Mark off his rhythm.

When the bell ended the second round and Lee headed to his corner, a small cut above his eyebrow was dripping blood. Catching his eye, Peggy shouted "stay strong!" Nodding to her, Lee saw she was holding his mother's hand. When he sat down, Big Hym tended his cut, trying to stop the bleeding.

"Remember, don't waste your energy," Father O'Connor said, giving him water. Save some to defend against his punches. Keep breathing and force him to move around the ring more. Wear him down. Throw a couple of hooks when you get the chance."

In the next three rounds, Lee and Mark both landed great punches. Mark hit Lee's body hard, but Lee countered by working Mark's ribs. When the bell ended the fifth round, both men were bruised. Lee looked tired as he walked to his corner, and his cut had opened again. When he sat down, Big Hym tried his best to stop the bleeding and used ice to slow the swelling in his face.

Getting in front of him, Father O'Connor said, "This is the last round, so expect him to swing harder. His legs are getting weak, so he might lean on you to help support his weight. If he does, push him off and keep working the body. Once his ribs are hurting and he lowers his arms, go for the hook. Listen, Lee, no matter what happens, I'm proud of you."

"You got this, brother," Big Hym said, and Father O'Connor put in his mouthpiece. In the final second before the bell, Lee lowered his head to catch his breath. When he did, his eyes caught the blue jay embroidered on the corner of his shorts. In that moment, he remembered Jack—not the fight that had resulted in Jack's death, but Jack's smile the first time he had shown him a drawing of a blue jay. Somehow, this image blocked out all of the noise, all of the doubt, all of the fear. When the bell rang, Lee looked determined.

Mark was also determined, however, and after blocking a few of Lee's punches, he landed some hard shots to Lee's head. Lee's cut had reopened, and a thin line of blood ran down the side of his face. His mother had her hands over her mouth, as if she were wondering whether she could take any more of this.

"Keep breathing!" Father O'Connor said. Lee did, and he began to hit Mark hard in the body. Mark seemed off balance, a sign his legs were getting weak. The fight became a brawl, as first Lee and then Mark drove the other to the ropes. Some in the crowd began to chant his new name— "Buddy! Buddy! Buddy!"—while others chanted Mark's name.

Lee kept moving as the two continued to exchange punches. Then, he saw his opening. He stepped back and jabbed with his left, and then he leaned forward and put his full force behind his right hook. The hook landed, and Mark fell to the canvas.

The crowd rose to their feet with a roar, as did Big Hym, Sam, and Father O'Connor. Standing over Mark, the referee began to count, "1... 2... 3... 4..." Lee walked to his corner, waiting to see whether Mark would get up. "9... 10!" the referee finished, waving his hands above his head to signal the match was over. Lee had won.

The crowd erupted. Everyone applauded, even those who had been chanting Mark's name, and many in the crowd jumped for joy. Big Hym climbed to the edge of the ring and parted the ropes, gesturing for Sam, Peggy, and Father O'Connor to enter. Peggy climbed through first and ran to meet Lee in the center of the ring. She threw her arms around him and gave him a long kiss on the lips. Soon, Father O'Connor, Sam, and Big Hym were there, too. Everyone hugged one another, elated. Then, Big Hym lifted Lee onto his shoulders, where he beamed over the crowd. The crowd resumed their chant of "Buddy, Buddy!" Smiling up at him, Father O'Connor winked and said, "Good job." Lee spotted his mother in the crowd, and she smiled and mouthed, "I love you!" Next to her, Gil and Roy smiled and applauded.

Jerry had made his way to the middle of the ring. He motioned to Lee and to Mark, who had regained consciousness, and they took their places on either side of him. "After six rounds," he boomed, "the winner of this contest is Buddy Lee! This is his first win as an amateur boxer!" At this, the crowd applauded and yelled for Lee once again. Before Mark left the ring, he hugged Lee and congratulated him on his victory.

Lee was escorted back to the locker room by his family and friends. As they walked, Father O'Connor put his arm around Lee's shoulder.

"That was the right hook!" he said. "I knew you had it in you!"

In the locker room, Doc awarded Lee his prize money. Lee left that night with five thousand dollars and a trophy.

# Chapter 16

A breakfast celebration at Father O'Connor's house had been planned for the next morning, but before Peggy and Lee said goodnight, they spent some time in the car outside of his mother's house. Peggy could not stop telling Lee how proud she was of him. She said while she could not fully comprehend the significance the fight must have had for him, she knew that God did, and that was all that mattered.

"In the last round, I felt I had won even before the bell rang," Lee said. "And I don't mean the fight. I felt as if I had won at life by embarking on this journey with God and realizing that He will always be with me."

"I'm elated for you, Lee," Peggy said.

Holding her hands in his own, he looked at her. "I have a question for you," he said.

"Sure. Ask me," she replied.

"Who is Buddy Lee?"

Peggy laughed aloud and then kept on laughing, as if she could not stop.

Watching her, Lee began to laugh as well. They laughed together for several minutes, until Peggy said, in her Irish accent, "Oh, I thought 'Buddy' sounded good with 'Lee,' so I put them together and came up with 'Buddy Lee!'"

She apologized to Lee, but he was not bothered one bit. Instead, he kissed her and said, "I love you."

"I love you, Buddy Lee," she said with a giggle.

"And the song you decided to play for me? Really?" They ended the night in a fit of uncontrollable laughter.

✝

The next morning, Lee got up early to help Peggy make breakfast. Big Hym and Sam had slept in, and he told them he would meet them at the O'Connor house in about an hour.

When Lee arrived, Peggy was the only one awake.

"Good morning, Lee. How's your body feeling?" she asked, hugging and kissing him.

"I'm a little sore, but okay," he said. "Are your parents and Father O'Connor still asleep?"

"Yes, I believe they are."

They walked into the kitchen, and Peggy began to take out some pans.

"Do you want me to start cooking some eggs?" Lee asked.

"You don't have to, Lee," she said, scanning the bruises on his face and the Band-Aid over his eyebrow.

Lee insisted he wanted to help, and Peggy relented. He removed the bacon and the eggs from the refrigerator while she put the pans on the stove.

"We make a good team, huh?" he said.

"We do," she replied, emptying some pancake mix into a bowl.

In a short while, they had prepared a wonderful breakfast.

Peggy started to set the table, and Lee took the orange juice from the refrigerator. Then, there was a knock at the door.

"I'll get it," Peggy said. It was Big Hym and Sam, and she told them to head into the kitchen. "Smells good!" Big Hym said.

Peggy went upstairs to tell her parents that breakfast was ready, and when she came down, she went to tell her uncle. She knocked on his door, but there was no answer. She entered slowly, but he was not in his room. Returning to the kitchen, she saw everyone but Father O'Connor. "Have you seen my uncle?" she asked Lee.

"No, I haven't," he said. "He wasn't in his room?"

"No." Peggy went outside to make sure his truck was in the driveway. It was not. When she came back in, Lee met her in the hallway.

"His truck isn't here," she said. "I wonder where he could be."

Lee thought for a moment, and then it came to him. "I think I know where he is," he said. "Go get the keys to your car, and I'll tell everyone we will be right back."

When she returned, they left immediately. Lee drove.

"Where are we going, Lee?" Peggy asked.

"He might be at the lake," Lee said. "I hope he is. He goes fishing there every Sunday."

✝

When they arrived at the lake a few minutes later, they saw Father O'Connor's truck and parked beside it.

"There he is!" Peggy said, pointing. He was in his usual spot, sitting in his chair with his Bible in his lap and his pole in its holder.

The lake was calmer than Lee had ever seen it. No wind disturbed the water and no birds made a sound.

"It's so beautiful here," Peggy said.

"It sure is," Lee replied.

As they walked towards Father O'Connor, they saw that his pole was bent. There was a fish on the line.

"Uncle, your fishing pole!" Peggy shouted as they began to run. They were excited to watch him catch a fish, especially since they had bought him the fishing pole for his birthday.

"Father O'Connor! I think you caught the big one!" Lee said, grabbing the pole from its holder.

"Reel it in, Lee!" Peggy shouted, standing next to him.

"I'm trying, but it's giving me a hard time!" Lee said. He reeled as fast as he could and jerked the rod upwards, but the fish responded with a stout tug. Finally, he was able to catch sight of it.

"I believe you got the right hook on this one," Lee said to Father O'Connor as he reeled in one of the biggest fishes he had ever seen.

"Wow! Uncle, you finally caught it!" Peggy said. In her excitement, she began shaking Father O'Connor's shoulder. "You caught it! You caught the big one!"

Lee lifted the fish out of the water, marveling at how heavy it was. Then, he turned around to show it to Father O'Connor.

"This was the right... hook..." he said, trailing off.

Peggy turned her eyes from Lee to Father O'Connor. Then, she saw the Bible on his lap. "Uncle! Uncle! Wake up, please! Uncle! Uncle!" she cried.

"Father O'Connor! Father! Wake up!" Lee said, trying to rouse him. Then, as he began to cry, his pleas gradually slowed. "Please... wake up..." he said.

Kneeling beside Father O'Connor's body, they hugged him and cried. Only their souls knew the pain they were experiencing. Father O'Connor had passed away in the chair that Sunday morning.

✝

At the funeral, another priest gave Father O'Connor's eulogy. As Lee surveyed the crowd, he was astonished at the number of people present. Lee finally realized why he was so special to everyone.

When the ceremony drew to a close, most stood in silence. Then, an elderly man in a wheelchair made his way to the coffin. In his hands was a small pair of boxing gloves, the kind people hung from their review mirrors. The man kissed the gloves, and then he laid them gently on the coffin. Although no one seemed to know who the gentleman was, they all sensed the importance of the gesture. Lee guessed the man's identity, however, and when he did, he began to cry.

As he cried, he recalled what he loved most about Father O'Connor: Father O'Connor was a man of God. The very first time Lee had met Father O'Connor, he had realized Father

O'Connor's relationship with God made him special. Lee had never met anyone who loved God as much as Father O'Connor had. Father O'Connor had lent him the tool he needed to fix the buffer and had trained him to box, but the most important gift he had given him was to teach him to always trust in the Lord. Lee knew now, more than ever, that Father O'Connor was right: God has a plan for everyone, and there is nothing we can do about His plans.

When everyone had paid their respects, Lee held Peggy's hand as they walked back to the car. On a nearby headstone, Lee saw two blue jays. They stopped walking to admire the birds, and Peggy put her head on his shoulder. Lee rested his head on top of hers. As a solitary tear rolled down his face, he whispered, "I'm going to miss him." Then, the birds flew away. Peggy used a tissue to wipe her eyes and nose.

They had almost reached her car when they heard footsteps behind them.

"Excuse me," someone said.

Turning, they saw a man in a suit. Peggy did not know the man, but Lee could not believe his eyes.

"I'm so sorry for your loss," the man said to Peggy. "I wanted to offer my condolences. Your uncle was a great man, and he meant a lot to me. He called me a couple of weeks ago to invite me to watch a young man with a great hook. I came because I knew your uncle and he was never wrong about people."

"Sorry," he said after a moment, extending his hand to Peggy. "I forgot to introduce myself. My name is Oscar De La Hoya."

"I know who you are," Lee said, shaking his hand, "but how did you know Father O'Connor?"

"When I was a young boxer, every week, Father O'Connor would visit the gym where I trained. He gave me advice about boxing, and more importantly, he gave me advice about my relationship with God."

Hearing this, Lee recalled the picture he had seen in the garage of Father O'Connor with Oscar De La Hoya.

"I wanted to tell you something, Lee," he continued. "I started an organization called Golden Boy Production a while back, and having seen you fight, I would be honored if you would join us as one of our boxers."

"I would love to!" Lee said, tearing up.

Peggy smiled and hugged him. "God is good!" she said.

Lee paused and responded a moment later. While looking up to the sky, he finally said "all the time."

The End

# About the Author

Larry Gaytan was born and raised in Lubbock, Texas. Larry graduated with a degree in education from Texas Tech University in 2009 and is a lifelong Red Raider fan.

He focuses his writing on fiction novels and children's book and would like to inspire children to follow their dreams no matter what life throws at them. He uses his own life as an example of how to do so.

In his writing, Larry hopes that readers understand that they're never alone, and wants his writing to inspire those struggling by helping them utilize their imagination and create a world of make believe.

In his spare time, Larry volunteers for a nonprofit organization feeding the homeless. His motto is “Everyone has a story to tell, why not you?”

# Acknowledgements

This book wouldn't be possible if it wasn't for the encouragement and support from many people. First of all, I would like to thank my family. To my daughters Esperanza, Alejandra and Galena Gaytan. I love y'all and I will always be here when you need me. To my mom and dad who are in heaven, I'm missing and loving y'all every day. To all my brothers and sister, you guys have been a blessing to me. To my nieces and nephews, I love y'all. To my aunts and uncles who passed away. To all of my cousins from both sides. To my cousins in Illinois, thank you for your hospitality when I was there.

To all my friends who supported me with my dream of becoming a writer. My thanks and appreciation goes out to KJ Waters for helping me put this book together.

To my friends Taha Habib and Robert Massengale, thank you for your support with helping me feed the flood victims and first responders in Kerrville, Texas.

To all the volunteers who helped me feed the homeless everywhere around Texas, I'm blessed to have you beside me. To the people of Boston, I appreciate you!

A special thanks to my readers who came out and supported me on my first book signing. To Rev. John G. Restrepo, O.P., I appreciate all the prayers and the talks that we had. To Sergio and Pricilla Mata, also Gerardo and Isela Mata in Kyle, Texas, thank you guys for your hospitality.

Can't forget Captain Peter Mata in San Benito, Texas and SGT Alcorte Leandro O., Dr Valerie A. Martinez, and David and

Ezekiel Gutierrez. To Meggie Hunter, thank you for your support and Kent Hance for your wisdom you shared with me.

To Jamie Chavez and Dr. Jose Molina, thanks for believing in me. To Jackie Chavez, thank you for pushing me through this process and I'm so grateful for all your help. To every trainer and boxer in the world who knows what it takes to become a champion in the ring.

To Sam Palacio, thanks for being there every time, better days are coming, my brother! Most importantly, I have to thank My Lord and Savior Jesus Christ. Without you in my life, this book wouldn't truly exist. Thank you for being my inspiration every day and constantly fighting my battles for me. I love you!

www.ingramcontent.com/pod-product-compliance
Lightning Source LLC
LaVergne TN
LVHW090534110826
845146LV00003B/1086